GW00838486

Apple Pie Order

42 Tales with a Twist

L. R. Longhurst

Raemark Press
Sedan, Kansas

Apple Pie Order: 42 Tales with a Twist
By L. R. Longhurst
Compiled and edited by Hazel Spire

ISBN: 978-1-7325090-2-3
LCCN: 2018956010

Published by Raemark Press
346 Road 21, Sedan, KS 67361
www.hazelspire.com

Front cover: 36 Victoria Road ~ photo by Hazel Spire
Back cover: LR.L. ~ photo by Joy Warren

Dedication

For Kath Longhurst

L. R. LONGHURST

Foreword

Transcribing and compiling APPLE PIE ORDER has been a labour of love and a team effort. Linda and I have fond memories of our father, Leslie Roy Longhurst, bashing out stories on his typewriter in the back rooms of 35 Fitzroy St. and 36 Victoria Rd, Sandown, Isle of Wight. In addition to working on reports and features for the *County Press*, Dad submitted short fiction as a freelance. It was thanks in part to his magazine credits that he'd landed the newspaper job. Mother wrote too, encouraged by Dad and a group of friends who met in our home. In 1966, after 12 summers of running a guest house (baking pies with home-grown blackberries and Bramley apples!) Mum embarked on her own journalistic career.

Some years after his passing, Dad's manuscripts and cuttings were divided among Linda, Nigel and me—Peter having died in 1978. We were amazed at the quantity and variety of stories. Whether murderous, humorous or romantic, all end with a sting or surprise. Conventions change, but there is still a place for good story-telling. Note the influence of O. Henry—innovator and master of the genre—whose name appeared on Dad's bookshelf next to Nevil Shute and C. S. Forester.

Nigel hand-bound a compilation of Dad's work, Volume I, for Mother's 85th birthday in 2013. While having hospital tests, he was keen to start on a second volume, but didn't live long enough to complete it. After I produced Volume II for a Longhurst reunion, on the centenary of Dad's birth, we found more stories that weren't in either one! It was time to put them together in paperback form—42 in all—not only for relatives but to reach a wider audience, both sides of the Atlantic.

I haven't attempted a chronology or theme divisions; the titles are arranged in alphabetical order—with one exception. "Winter Comes Too Soon" should be placed earlier but seems best suited for the end. Two or three manuscripts were partially hand-written; L.R.L. had made notes in the margins, intending to elaborate. Nigel and I used editorial licence in the final shaping, yet with few changes necessary.

Although the book is printed in America, I retained British spelling and usage. Thanks to Linda for her help with editing. We are extremely grateful for our literary legacy and the joys of family life in our house by the sea. ~ H.S.

L. R. LONGHURST

PAGE/STORY TITLE   PUBLICATION CREDITS

Apple Pie Order

Whenever I hear it said that there's no sentiment in business, I am reminded of Edgar J. Westry, the catering king. In particular I think of the episode of Old Mother Dumpling and the Carchester College tuckshop.

This is the story as recounted to me (somewhat apologetically, I may say) by the great Edgar J. himself: Chancing to have a spare half-an-hour while in Carchester on business, Westry slipped into the grounds of the college he had left some 25 years ago. As was only to be expected, buildings which had once towered over him seemed to have been dwarfed by time; indeed, the lush green quadrangle was no bigger than the lawn of his country house. But Westry soon discovered that what the place had lost in stature it had gained in atmosphere, which enveloped him in a rosy old-world glow. Since leaving the college he had side-stepped all invitations to reunion gatherings—too busy building up businesses, he had always pleaded. Now he congratulated himself on the whim which had led him to shake hands once again with tradition.

Tradition, in the shape of old Duggins, the school janitor, welcomed him with open arms. Westry bumped into those arms as he stepped back sharply after admiring a cloistered chapel.

"Good morning, Mr. Westry, sir," said the old man heartily. "I wondered when you was coming back!"

Westry, who rubbed shoulders daily with financial wizards and city magnates, was strangely thrilled at recognition from this humble quarter. "Why, Duggins, how remarkable that you should still remember me."

"Not at all, sir. Your picture is so often in the papers I can't hardly forget you. Though mark you, Mr. Westry," he added confidentially, "with due respects, I always thinks of you as the Encyclopedia of the Fourth."

Again, Westry thrilled at this reminder of the nickname. As an inquisitive fourth-former, he had sought to learn all he could about everything and everybody, and he had been equally ready to pass on information to all and sundry. Hence the title, the Encyclopedia of the Fourth, which had followed him through to his sixth-form days.

Reluctantly, the janitor looked at his watch. "If you will excuse me, sir, I must ring the bell for morning break. I hope you'll look me up in my lodge some time."

"And I, too, must be going, Duggins—urgent appointment—but I'll see you again soon."

The urgent appointment which Edgar J. Westry had suddenly remembered was not a business one; it was simply that he had a sudden urge to visit the tuckshop close to the school grounds to witness once again the mad, joyous scramble for chairs during morning break. It had also occurred to him (to bring his "encyclopedia" up to date) to learn whether Old Mother Dumpling still held sovereignty behind the counter.

She did. The generous curves which had prompted the nickname were un-deflated by time, and her friendly smile was equally as outsize. Greying hair, and a certain slowness of movement, alone recorded the passing of the years.

Westry perched his own cumbersome figure somewhat uncertainly on a high stool, and having gained his equilibrium, ordered a ginger pop and a doughnut. His stomach gave a warning gurgle, and he hastily amended the order to an orange squash and a slice of cake.

"Look here, sir," the good lady declared, "I'll make you a cup of tea. I'm not over-busy, as you can see."

As a matter of fact, Westry was the sole customer, which he thought was odd. When the nice cup of tea had been brought to him, he asked, "Where are all the lads?"

Old Mother Dumpling sighed. "They go to the Ace café, a little way down the road. Seeing as it's a new place, all plush-and-chromium-like, I can't hold the custom."

Westry tut-tutted. "I should have thought your home-made apple pies would have done the trick."

"Alas!" replied the old lady. "I don't make 'em nowadays. I'm not so steady on me pins."

Westry drank his tea in reflective sips. Suddenly he was inspired to open his briefcase, and from amid a welter of documents he took out an odd-looking parcel. Removing the cellophane wrapping, he handed the article to the old lady. "There you are, Mother! The tastiest apple pie in the kingdom!"

Old Mother Dumpling cut the pie and sampled the taste. "Umm," she murmured. "It's delicious."

"It's a new line," Westry explained, "and one of my companies supplies the pie. If you would like the sole concession, I could arrange a daily delivery to Carchester for you. What d'you say?"

"I'd say bless you, sir."

"Don't bless me, madam, bless tradition."

When telling me the story later, Edgar J. said he had been tempted at first to advertise the new pie for Old Mother Dumpling on a commercial scale—with glaring streamers and publicity blurbs. Then he had realised that ostentation would not be in keeping with his newly acquired respect for tradition. Instead, he went straight away back to the college, and knocked at the janitor's lodge.

"I came back sooner than you expected, Duggins, because I'd like you to do something for me."

"I'm always ready to oblige my gentlemen," said the janitor, "as you may well remember, sir."

"I do, indeed. Tell me, who is the present-day school encyclopedia?"

The janitor beamed broadly. "Why, Nosey Noggs, sir. A prairie fire couldn't spread quicker than his news!"

Westry produced a pound note. "This will remind you to ask Nosey Noggs to tell all his friends to call at Old Mother Dumpling's tuckshop—where they will eat something to their advantage."

"Thank you kindly, sir. I'll nab young Nosey right away."

Thanks to the modern encyclopedia, within a few days hundreds of schoolboys were flocking to the tuckshop, jostling their way to the counter to sample Old Mother Dumpling's delicious apple pies. Before the month was up, the plush-and-chromium Ace café had been obliged to move to another town.

There's no sentiment in business, d'you say? I'll take you up on that point. You see, I am manager of the Ace café. What is more (as Edgar J. Westry somewhat apologetically told me), the new line in apple pies which set the tuckshop back on its traditional footing was originally intended for the Ace café.

The Ace café is one of Westry's many businesses.

Bad Show!

If there's one thing I pride myself on—and in fact there are dozens—it's a memory for faces. If there's another thing I pride myself on, it's a memory for names. The snag is I find it difficult to fit the right name to the right face.

I can reel off a whole string of names at any time—Smith, Jones, Brown, Robinson, Chiverton, Cheverton, Attrill, and so on. And I can recall some really outstanding faces—ugly, pretty, pretty ugly, bearded wonders, moustachioed miracles, spotty, wrinkled or warted. But to correlate the conk with the cognomen, the handle with the handlebar moustache, is another matter.

My constant endeavour to name-fit a face becomes a matter of two-fold pride: my pride in demonstrating a good memory and a general interest in the welfare of others; and the pride of the recognisee in the knowledge that they are really someone. *But who are they?* I ask myself before shaking their hands or inquiring after their health and that of their wives and children. Because for the life of me I can seldom remember if they are married or, if so, whether the union was blessed with progeny.

A case in point: I was travelling from Newport to Ryde the other day, and on the bus was a familiar face with a name that for the moment escapes me. It escaped me at that moment, too.

"Good morning," said the face.

"Good morning, Mr. Er-um," I said, and hastily drowned the remark in a cough and busied myself in settling in a seat beside the face.

"How's things with you?" asked the face.

"Fine," I replied.

"Good show!" he said.

The expression on his anonymous features indicated that, having displayed such an extra-ordinary interest in my welfare, my companion expected me to inquire after his.

It might have helped if I knew where he lived. But since he was travelling from Newport, that cosmopolitan centre of the Island's life, he might reside anywhere in the Island. And even if he did live in Newport, so did 19,879 other faces. The fact that he was travelling to Ryde told me little, other than that he was obviously going to catch a boat, because he was spruced up to the nines and a large suitcase was tucked under the seat.

I tried an exploratory shot.

"How did your last show go down?"

I knew I was on fairly safe ground here. There must be more societies and organisations to the square inch in the Isle of Wight than anywhere else in Great Britain, and nearly everyone belongs to one or the other. The noun "show" was artfully selected. It could refer to a horticultural show, cage bird show, dog show, cat show, art exhibition, theatrical production, or even, in the broad sense, to a darts contest or a football match. And, in the broadest sense, to a coffee morning or a jumble sale.

"The show," replied the face. "Oh, it went down very well. There was a record attendance."

That did not help much. Nearly every show in the Island attracts a record attendance, judging by the reports of enthusiastic secretaries.

"Good show!" I commented.

"Yes, it was a good show. The judges said the quality was as good as anything on the mainland."

I never heard of a judge who did not say that, so we hadn't got much farther. Except that the field was narrowed to a show of the competitive exhibition type. That ruled out football and darts matches, coffee mornings and jumble sales.

"Who won the cup for most points?" I asked. (There was just a chance I might remember my face's name if I knew someone else in the same outfit.)

"Oh, that was won by the same fellow as last year."

"Who," I asked desperately, "was runner-up?" Surely a name— any name—would be divulged.

The face replied, "I was."

"Good show!" I said.

Not a very enlightening conversation, you may well think. But at least to date I had saved our mutual embarrassment in not having to reveal that I did not know his name. Outwardly nonchalant, mentally I perspired freely as I racked my brain for a name to fit the Bill—or Tom, or Dick, or Harry.

I fumbled with cigarettes and matches for the multi-purpose of providing breathing space, eating up the journey to Ryde in silence, and providing fuel for the brainbox. I tied and re-tied shoelaces, commented freely on matters of scenic interest which did not call for a knowledge of my companion's name, and I even sank to zero level by discussing the weather.

When Ryde Esplanade hove in sight I breathed more freely. Another Er-um by way of parting greeting might yet save our mutual bacon, providing it was judiciously disguised by a cough. The bus stopped and the face got up to go.

"Cheerio," I said loudly and proudly, "Cheerio, Mr. Witherspoon." The bacon had been saved by a closer glance at his suitcase, on which the name was blazoned in gilt letters.

"Cheerio," Mr. Witherspoon replied. "Cheerio, Mr. Er-um."

Bashful Types

"Don't look now," said the pretty W.R.A.F. "But that's my boyfriend over there. He's terribly jealous."

Up to that moment Lance-Corporal George Waverton had been enjoying the Forces dance in the company of the friendliest, most charming girl he had ever met. But now he stopped suddenly in mid dance step, stubbing his partner's dainty toe in the process.

He swivelled his head in the general direction of Pamela's glance, to where a group of wallflowering soldiery were assembled in the corner of the hall.

One warrior stood literally head and shoulders above the rest—six foot six inches of militant muscularity.

George gulped. "Your ex-boyfriend, eh? Jealous, you say?"

The band struck up with "Two lovely black eyes"—ominously topical, George thought as he hastily directed his partner to the opposite end of the hall. Opposite to where the six-foot-sixer stood as if on sentry-go.

"Don't panic, darling," Pamela murmured. "Cuthbert is really quite the bashful type."

"Cuthbert! Do they actually call him Cuthbert?"

"Well, yes, but his Army pals call him the Basher."

George nodded glumly. "Don't wonder at it. But I thought you said he was the bashful type."

"He must be bashful," Pamela pointed out bashfully, "if they call him the Basher. Incidentally, he's the Unit champion."

"Let's go for a coffee."

"Later, darling. I do believe you're scared."

"Of course I'm not scared," George declared with what he hoped was assurance. The band stopped playing but he continued dancing. Out in the middle of the floor he was safe from the most jealous and muscular of wallflowers.

A few people started clapping, imagining this was an exhibition dance. Pamela whispered urgently, "Stop! There's no need to make us both look foolish just because you're scared."

"Of course I'm not scared," George repeated. Goaded into rashness, he added, "You see! I'll go up and speak to your precious basher!"

With determined steps—in case he changed his mind—George strode towards the fateful corner. He elbowed aside a knot of hangers-on and stood before the giant.

He eyed the big man up and down—slowly, deliberately. Then he spoke. "Hello, Cuthbert!"

When George's head cleared later, he had to admit that his ill-advised remark had been more of a jeer than a greeting. The big man must have thought the same, for his return was a power-packed precision punch to the point of George's jaw.

Dimly, from his uncomfortable position on the floor, the victim was aware of Pamela bending over him, murmuring sweet nothings, and George thought that perhaps it was all worthwhile.

Actually the sweet nothings were quite somethings. "You're a chump," Pamela was saying. "But I love you all the more for your mistake. *You spoke to the wrong man.* That's Cuthbert, next to the fellow that hit you."

George raised his aching head. The young man next to the giant was of weedier proportions, around the 5-foot-8 mark.

"So that's Cuthbert," George said ruefully, rising unsteadily to his feet. "I can imagine him being bashful, but it beats me why they call him the Basher. A Unit champion at that, you say."

Pamela led George away for that much-needed coffee, and explained with a disarming smile. "Cuthbert can peel a potato quicker than anyone in the battalion. He's the Unit's champion Spud Basher."

Bedside Watch

Racked with a fever that in a younger man would have stopped at a three-day 'flu, Wilberforce Braydon tossed and turned in the hard hospital bed.

The voice of Nurse Brookes cut through the mists of his subconscious. "Mr. Braydon, there's two gentlemen to see you." The announcement was charged with a barely-suppressed excitement.

He opened his pale-blue eyes, but the line of his vision did not stray beyond the dressing gown on his bedside cabinet. Where was his three-piece suit? The new black-and-white pinstripe, with the all-important waistcoat.

Still, what did it matter now? What did anything matter?

He closed his eyes again, blotting out the anxious glances of the nurse and the two visitors.

The bedside conversation merged with this delirium. "I'd better not wake him," Nurse Brookes said. "But you can wait here, in case he wakes on his own. He needs visitors desperately."

His head, in its contortions, splayed the pillow with tousled, tinselled strands. The bushy tufts of eyebrow, and the straggly moustache, were of the same bright silver.

The nurse smoothed the pillow and soothed his brow. Then she studied the chart at the foot of the bed and shook her head. What had robbed the funny little man of his will to live?

The two visitors caught the concern in the nurse's eye, and they exchanged glances. "Old Braydon was as fit as a fiddle a week ago," said one. "I just don't understand it."

"Listen," said his companion. "He's trying to say something."

"Delirious," said the other man curtly.

They leaned forward to glean sheaves of sense from the muttered mumbo jumbo....

Wilberforce Braydon had joined the family firm of Waters and Son as a lad of fifteen. He started as a book-keeper (being entrusted

APPLE PIE ORDER: 42 TALES WITH A TWIST

with the postage book) and 50 years later was still a book-keeper.

The measure of his responsibility had increased over the years, for the books he kept were the sales and bought ledgers; but he had never really made his mark in the commercial world. He had failed to expand with the firm.

Juniors were appointed over his head—notably George Rigby, ten years younger than Braydon; as chief accountant Rigby was now his immediate boss.

Perhaps, had Braydon married, he would have been encouraged to move with the times. But he had been jilted while serving in France in the First World War, and had retreated into his bachelor shell.

He had made his mark in other directions, however—such as in loyalty of service, sharp time keeping, and a kindly disposition which had earned the respect, while not perhaps the friendship, of all his colleagues.

With all its expansion the firm still retained the family touch, and the managing director, bluff Bruce Waters, made a feature of presentations.

It was customary for an employee who had served the company for 50 years or one who was due for retirement after long service, to receive a handsome inscribed gold watch.

Wilberforce Braydon came into both categories, since his retirement coincided with a half-century of service.

The normal retirement age was 65. Only men specially invited by the management were given a 70-year option. Braydon had not been asked to stay on a further five years.

He was sorry about this, because book-keeping was his life. His outside interests were few, and his home life was bounded by the fireside chair, the television set, and the products of the local library.

As retirement day drew near, however, he resigned himself to the new life, and the fresh horizons would be marked by the gold watch he was to receive. Often he would daydream in the office (after he had balanced the books for the day, of course) on his retirement routine.

At ten o'clock in the morning, for instance, he would be able to look at his gold watch, and if the weather was fine he would stroll through the park and read his newspaper on the bench which caught the most sun.

He could imagine a youngster approaching him, wanting to know the right time. He would proudly pull out his gold watch and, before imparting the desired knowledge, would say, "See here, my boy, this is what Messrs. Waters and Son, the well-known timber importers, gave me for 50 years' loyal service. You can earn the same mark of esteem one day if you put your mind to it."

After that, he decided, he would consult his watch at intervals, and when it registered 11:30, say, he would move on to the Liberal Club where one or two of his acquaintances used to gather.

Then, after a game of chess, he would consult his watch as lunch-time approached—thus affording an opportunity to tell his fellow clubmen of the signal honour bestowed upon him by the esteemed family firm.

So the daydream reached its climax on the day of his 65th birthday, which coincided with the end of the week—pay day and PRESENTATION DAY. (The words were written in capital letters in his mind.)

It was a dream no longer now. He was actually living the experience. He dressed extra smartly that day, putting on his new three-piece black-and-white pin-stripe suit. Normally he wore a two-piece, with a thick woollen cardigan. But a waistcoat was essential now; he needed a pocket to put the watch in.

At the end of the day he received the expected summons to the managing director's office, his heart pumping a rhythm to his racing thoughts. The sad prospect of leaving the firm to which he had devoted his life was largely compensated by the pocketable mark of their esteem which he was soon to receive.

Some twenty or thirty staff had gathered in Bruce Waters' sanctum, glasses filled ready to toast the health and happiness of the popular little book-keeper.

Somehow, Wilberforce contrived a calm he could not possibly feel. Unobtrusively, he unfastened his jacket button, so that the waistcoat was exposed.

Mr. Waters was making a speech, but Braydon did not hear a word; he was slyly peering over the edge of the desk to catch a glimpse of the gold watch.

While Waters was speaking, the crowd of humanity in the office opened up, and the object in the corner of the room could be clearly seen. A handsome inscribed grandfather clock.

Wilberforce Braydon buttoned up his jacket again. The action was not only practical but symbolic. He was buttoning up his daydreams, and the glorious life he had earmarked for himself in retirement.

How could he take this monster of a grandfather clock to the park? Or to the club? The hall of his little flat was the only place for it, but he did not expect to receive any visitors to whom he could relate the signal honour his firm had bestowed upon him.

The hum of anticipation in the office changed to consternation, as Braydon fell forward in a faint.

There had been a nip in the air that day, and because he had discarded his woollen cardigan Braydon caught a chill. Although he was rushed to the hospital, the chill soon turned to pneumonia.

He made no effort to resist it....

The two visitors watched anxiously as Wilberforce Braydon tossed and turned.

Then George Rigby said, "Look, he's waking!"

Braydon opened his eyes and gave a wan smile as he recognised his chief accountant and managing director.

"A fine one you are," said Waters. "Fainting in the middle of my speech the other day."

"I'm sorry, sir," Braydon quavered, with dull politeness.

Waters chuckled. "Never mind, but you missed the most important part. I was just about to tell you that the clock was a special present for 50 years' outstanding service. We want you stay on another five years, after which, incidentally, you will qualify for a gold watch."

Braydon beamed—an outsize smile, which indicated that Nurse Brookes would soon be able to throw her chart away.

Outside the hospital, the chief accountant said, "Now we'd better dash back to the office, sir. My secretary was sending off Braydon's cards today. We'll have to stop them."

Bluff Bruce Waters gave an approving wink.

Chequered Careers

The day I interviewed Jasmine Jaques, the renowned novelist, was fraught with surprises.

In the first place, it was unusual for the author to grant the press audience. Since rocketing to fame with *Honeysuckle and Roses*, she had avoided the glare of publicity; and hiding her light under a bushel had thrived in its shadow.

In the second place, the most loyal employee would not claim the *Clayford Herald* to be other than a humble journal, rarely selected to spotlight celebrities.

In the third place, I had always criticised Jasmine Jaques' works unmercifully in my book review column, dismissing them caustically as the slobberingly sentimental.

In the fourth, fifth and sixth places... well, this brings me to the threshold of the author's villa, the door being opened to me by a trim young lady. "Miss Jasmine Jaques?" I asked, presenting my card. She denied the charge with a cryptic smile, leading me straightaway into a well-appointed study.

"I'm Miss Hilton, her secretary. Do make yourself comfortable while I call Miss Jaques."

I sank into an easy chair and drank in ravenously the sparkling air of luxury all around me. Every fixture and fitting underlined the author's success: the bulging bookshelves, the tempting cocktail cabinet, and the thick pile carpet, to walk upon which was akin to crossing the Goodwin Sands.

I must confess that the chief reaction was one of envy. If only, I mused, I'd had the breaks that are said to be essential to a successful writer; or if only I had made full use of the few breaks which had come my way....

My train of thought was halted; it was the entry of Miss Hilton that had pulled the communication cord. "Miss Jaques won't be long," she said, "but she suggests you might like to go ahead with your story. You can use my typewriter on the desk there if you wish.

As for material, if you study the two photo frames on the desk, you will have all the copy you require."

This being obviously one of those days, I took this Alice-in-Wonderland-ish development in my stride; and seated at the author's desk, I looked for the clues mentioned. In the larger frame was the portrait of a man of about my own age (assuming this to be a recent photograph); and across the photo was scrawled the information: "Raymond Ward, alias Jasmine Jaques." So! The purveyor of what I termed undiluted tripe was a man!

The smaller frame contained a cheque, dated ten years back, for the sum of £200.

Miss Hilton had been right. It was possible to work out a story, and with only the minimum of head-scratching, I was soon hammering away at the keys.

Jasmine Jaques, I wrote, *was introduced to the Registrar of Births and Deaths as Raymond Ward: Jasmine was an infant of his imagination not to see the light of day for a further 25 years.*

Whilst not of straitened means, Raymond's parents were by no means affluent; but with an aptitude for study, he passed a succession of scholarships through Grammar School, Public School and University. There he studied for the Bar but his heart was never really in the Legal Profession. Eventually Literature wooed and won him, and coming down from the University he took a flat in Chelsea, in an effort to set the world of letters afire. For a long time, however, he produced nothing more than a mild spark.

During this rather unsatisfactory phase, he met up with a struggling literary twin soul. Arthur Radley. Radley, too, found the Path of Prose a thorny one, and jointly they collected so many rejection slips they could have promoted their own Paper Chases.

Though the two had so much in common there was this contrast in personality: Raymond Ward was ever the businessman, Arthur Radley the dreamer.

With consummate skill, Ward budgeted for their frugal needs on the proceeds of two slender incomes and an occasionally successful article. Radley, the dreamer, acted as morale-booster. The world was theirs for the asking, Radley constantly reiterated, if only they were to persevere.

A favourite talking point was the great day when they were to have a major work accepted. They both averred that when their first big cheque arrived they would frame it as a spur to greater things.

The great day arrived in the shape of a national novel competition for new writing. Raymond Ward won the first prize of £200, whilst Arthur Radley had an honourable mention worth £50. Before the results were announced, however, their paths had separated, Radley being called up North on family business.

I had got so far on my story, when Raymond Ward, the famous author in person, entered the room, and greeted me warmly. "Hello, Arthur Radley, it is good to see you again. Moving into the district and hearing you were with *The Herald*, I planned this surprise. Well, what have you made of my life?"

I showed him my notes which he read with interest.

"I observe you won a £50 prize," he said. "Did it spur you on to greater things?"

"Unfortunately not," I replied sadly. "The cheque stands framed on my desk to this day; but for all the good it did me, I might as well have cashed it. But I was ever the dreamer."

"Hard luck!" Ward commiserated. "Now my £200 *did* lead to better things. With the proceeds I rented a cottage in the country in idyllic surroundings and changed my style to the one you so strongly condemn, but one which has reaped the dividends. In six months, *Honeysuckle and Roses* was born."

"Hold on a moment," I exclaimed. "How could you have spent the proceeds, when the cheque stands framed there on your desk?"

Raymond Ward smiled. "The framed edition is a photostat copy; it serves the same purpose and is more economical. As you say, I was ever the businessman."

Destination Dynasty

The biggest curiosity in Robbley's curio shop was Robbley. But not in the antiquated sense, for Raymond Robbley was not the shuffling, shabby antique dealer favoured by the cartoonists, but an athletic, ex-R.A.F. type in his early forties.

Away from his dingy shop in the Charing Cross Road you might take him to be a successful motor-car salesman. As it happened, he had been just that at one time, earning more in commission than many of his clients who bought glamorous limousines on glamorous hire-purchase terms.

When an uncle bequeathed to him the curio shop, his pals advised him to "Flog it, old chap."

Objay darts, they told him in shaky French but sound logic, were not in his line.

But seizing the chance to climb out of a post-war rut, Robbley had taken over the shop with eccentric gusto, and in fifteen years he had made it pay.

You might think that a man of his type would know nothing about antiques, curios, and works of art. And you would be right. But where expert knowledge was lacking, instinct came to the rescue.

In any case, as he told the scoffers, he was not so much interested in fat profits—though he did not scorn them—as in the story behind the curio.

The painted lampshade was a case in point. Robbley's hunch told him to buy it as soon as it was laid in the counter by the man who looked to be down on his luck. Robbley did not think much of the bedside lamp as a piece of furniture, ornament or *objet d'art*. Neither did he think his clients would rave about it.

So he immediately took it to pieces. The short wooden tubular support he diagnosed as cheap cedar. The circular base was of a material in the alabaster family; discoloured and distinguished only by an inscription underneath. The print was barely decipherable, but he could just about make out the lettering, in quarter-of-an-inch capitals, MING.

For all his ignorance to the finer points of antiques, Robbley had heard of the Ming dynasty and the value of its products. But he also knew that the ancient Chinese did not make a point of publicising their work in English!

He assumed that the name had been printed by someone out to make an easy profit from a gullible collector—not necessarily by the client who now stood anxiously on the other side of the counter. He seemed too genuine for that.

At an impulse Robbley flung the piece into a corner, where a pile of unsaleable junk awaited dispatch to the scrap merchant.

The agitated client said, "Hey, you'll have to buy it now!"

Robbley smiled disarmingly. "Don't worry, chum. I've already decided to do so." He pointed to the lampshade. "This is the part which interests me."

It was made of a plain parchment, but enlivened by the painting of an Oriental scene—a mosque and minaret, a palm tree and, in the background, a train of camels. Not a work of art; but Robbley had an idea he could make something attractive out of it.

"How much are you asking for it?"

"Twenty-five bob. I gave three quid for it, now."

Robbley surveyed his client, assessing the degree of his need. "I only deal in round figures," he replied.

"All right, then. Say a quid."

Robbley grinned. "I had five pounds in mind."

His client whistled. "Thanks, pal, you're a toff."

"Before you go," said Robbley, "there's just a formality. If you can prove ownership of the lamp, it would help. A receipt, perhaps?"

For the first time during the interview, the client smiled and his eyes lit up as his mind flashed back to the distant scene depicted by the lampshade.

"That's rich! They don't hand out receipts in the bazaars of Cairo."

Cairo! The name set Robbley's own memory travels in motion. He dashed to the other side of the counter, muttered, "Don't go away," and ran out of the shop.

He was soon back, bearing two cups of black coffee. "Let's finish the deal Arab fashion," he said. "Perch yourself on that chair and have a cigarette. Bought 'em specially. Turkish.

"Now," he continued when the preliminaries were over, "where exactly in Cairo did you buy the lamp?"

"In the big bazaar near the Cinema Mabruk. The end shop, run by Abu Shawarib. Know him?"

"Abu Shawarib—Father of the Moustaches!" Robbley exclaimed. "All our R.A.F. mob knew him. He gave some useful hints on moustache cultivation! I bought most of my coming-home presents at his shop."

"Well, old chap, I think you've made out a case for ownership, and here's your money." Robbley counted out the notes. "Three, four, five, and, ah, one more for old times' sake."

When his client had gone he took the lampshade to pieces, removing the wire supports, top and bottom, and slitting the join—so that he had a long, flat-surfaced painting. Then he trimmed the edges parallel with a knife. In the little workshop behind the counter, he made a simple frame for the picture and hung it on the wall of the shop.

The finished product was of unusual shape and hardly in the masterpiece class—but was this not a curio shop?

The picture hung for several weeks, collecting the dust of ages and the scathing remarks of connoisseurs. Until the prosperous American came into the shop. He was no connoisseur, but he knew what he liked. And he liked the Oriental painting.

"I'll give you a hundred dollars for it," he said.

"Pounds," said Robbley—who cut the cloth of his prices according to the cut of his clients' clothes.

"It's a deal. I'll take two of them."

Robbley explained that his was an antique shop, not a multiple store.

The American was disappointed but obdurate. "There must be another in existence somewhere," he said. "You find a picture to match that one and I'll give you a thousand dollars for the two."

"Pounds," said Robbley.

"It's a deal."

Now Robbley was a firm believer in the impossible. So he ushered out his client with instructions to call back at the end of the week. Already a scheme was bubbling over in his effervescent mind.

He would fly to Cairo, call at the shop of Abu Shawarib and buy another painted lampshade. And he would go by the first available plane.

The next day he shut up shop, posting a typically-cryptical note in the window: "Gone hunting. Normal business will be resumed as soon as possible."

He realised that his journey was not strictly necessary. He could arrange to have the Oriental scene duplicated without leaving London. But he regarded the affair as a challenge. For a true match—and nothing less would satisfy him—he must seek the original merchant, or if necessary the actual maker of the lampshade.

Cairo was in many respects the same city he had known during the war; except that amid the hustle and bustle of the bazaars he missed the hordes of British soldiery bargaining in their peculiar brand of pidgin Arabic.

The Oriental perfumes were there; Nostalgia with a capital sniff. The romantic Middle East—in the sense that his own curio shop was romantic; dingy in parts, but colourful and out of the ordinary.

Robbley found Abu Shawarib's shop without difficulty, but there he met his first setback. He of the flowing robes and the flowing moustaches was absent. In his place was a younger edition in Western dress, with a more trim moustache.

Robbley showed him the painting and explained about the lampshade. Would the son of the Father of the Moustaches by chance have another in stock?

"Lampshade? No, those we do not sell today. But we have some exceedingly excellent filigree bracelets."

Robbley shook his head.

"Then perhaps a mother-of-pearl cigarette box?"

At any other time Robbley might have considered ordering stock for his shop, but at the moment he was not to be put off the lampshade track.

"Perhaps you recall where you bought them?"

"Alas, no. During the war I was too young to take an interest in the business."

"How long has your father been dead?"

The Arab smiled. "My father is still alive, *Alhamdulillah*. He rests now from the afternoon sun. But I will call him."

Robbley's hopes soared again.

At his son's bidding old Abu Shawarib tottered into the shop. His moustaches were as handsome as ever, although silvery now; and the head under the *hatta* and e*gal*—which was somewhat askew—was completely bald.

"*Ahlan wa sahlan*," he greeted Robbley. "A thousand welcomes." To his son he gave an instruction in Arabic, and Robbley gathered he was asking for the coffee to be brought.

The old man drew up the chairs, toppling a pile of pigskin suitcases to make more room.

Not until the cigarettes were smoked and the first cup of coffee consumed did the old gentleman introduce the subject of business. His son translated Robbley's request.

Robbley watched anxiously as Abu Shawarib's perplexity changed to understanding. Then he burst into a torrent of Arabic.

The younger Arab translated. "My father says he recalls the origin of the lampshades. They came from a very honourable merchant in a far country, and my father will find you the address so that you may seek him out."

The old man cut short his thanks, so Robbley bought a pigskin suitcase.

He hurried back to London, to telephone a progress report to the American client's hotel.

Then he set out on the onerous journey to the merchant in a far country. He had little doubt now that he would be able to match the painting. The rigours of the journey before him were compensated by the triumph of a challenge successfully met.

As the train steamed out of Euston station, Robbley realised what the full inscription of the lampshade base was, before worn away by time: MADE IN BIRMINGHAM.

Dinner for One

With a grunt of relief, Gregory Marlowe sidled into a seat on the tube train. He wanted to think; and he could hardly do so in the strap-hanging position, with an umbrella poking him in the ribs on one side and a newspaper fanning his ear on the other.

He had left the office on the stroke of 5:30, so anxious was he to erase all thoughts of his quarrel with Margaret that morning, before it qualified for the "unpleasant memory" class. Of recent months he had collected too many mental souvenirs of stormy domestic scenes, and he didn't want to add to the collection.

This unhappy state of affairs, mainly a bickering over trifles, had been punctuated at intervals by the departure of his wife, who at these times of crisis would stay with her mother. The one bright spot was that she always came back—the return being marked by mutual reproaches and renewed affection.

The current quarrel had centred on the mother-in-law theme. "Dig out your finery today," Gregory had warned Margaret at the breakfast table. "We're going to a dance tonight."

A surprise of this sort was calculated to please his wife, but this time she had damped his enthusiasm with a blank refusal. "I'm worried about Mother," Margaret had replied. "She was none too well yesterday, so I simply *must* see her tonight."

Upon reflection now, Gregory was ready to admit that Margaret had been right, especially as her sister Hilda—who lived with their mother—was away. He also admitted, secretly, that his mother-in-law was a good old soul, by no means a marriage-wrecker. But on leaving home that morning he had stated the reverse opinion, giving force to his remarks by slamming the door behind him and forgoing the farewell embrace.

He'd had a wretched day at the office, and he hoped he would be home in time to put things right with Margaret before she went to see her mother. Imbued with a sense of urgency, he alighted from the train and dashed through the barrier with such abandon that the inspector called him back to check his ticket.

Out in the street at last, he walked at an uncomfortably sharp pace, jumbled phrases of apology and endearment wrestling in his mind for the honour of first place on his lips.

He need not have rehearsed them. When he opened his street door he was met only by a silence which to his taut nerves held the quality of an uncanny cathedral calm. Margaret had gone already! Now he would have to wait hours with the words unspoken.

"Pull yourself together, old chap," he muttered. "It's a blow, but not a tragedy."

Adopting a false air of casualness, he went into the dining-room; but there was not so much as a cold meal prepared for him. He drew a blank in the kitchen, too. Now this was surprising: on the last occasion Margaret had gone away she had bequeathed him a skeleton pantry, and taken to task on her return had promised never to let it happen again. Something must be seriously amiss for Margaret to break her word.

Foraging in the larder, Gregory managed to concoct a makeshift meal of sandwiches and biscuits, which he ate with an air of ever-mounting foreboding. It was hopeless; he couldn't finish the meal, for the food stuck in his throat. So he went into the lounge and switched on the radio. The variety programme might well have lulled him back to a more cheerful frame of mind... had not the hearty comedian introduced some gags on the mother-in-law theme. Gregory switched off, savagely.

Then he saw the note on the mantelpiece. It was in Margaret's handwriting, scrawled in the margin of a scrap of magazine page. It was short, but *not* sweet. It had the same urgency, and the same lack of punctuation, as a curt telegram:

GONE TO MOTHER'S AS I SAID I WOULD

BUT THIS TIME I'M LEAVING

So! This was the end. Gregory read the note a score of times, trying to read, between the lines, sentiments which obviously weren't there. And he would have read on indefinitely had not the gathering dusk closed in on him, to harmonise in a minor key with his despondent mood.

The irony of the situation taunted him. Just as he had been about to adopt a spirit of more-give and less-take, the chance had been denied him. *Or had it?* he asked himself suddenly. Why should he let Margaret go so easily when there was a telephone in the hall? True, his mother-in-law had no telephone; but her neighbour, Vernon Baxley, was a good sort. Baxley would call in Margaret to the phone.

Gregory dialled Baxley's number, and within a matter of seconds the receiver at the other end was picked up. "Hello, who's speaking?" asked a silvery voice. Slowly, Gregory replaced his receiver, without answering. The silvery voice belonged to Margaret.

The situation was now perfectly clear—Margaret had left him for Vernon Baxley. Thus were her frequent visits to Mother explained. And what a convenient base for operations was the house next door to her clandestine lover!

Gregory switched off the hall light and groped his way back into the lounge. He sat down in an easy chair, but there was no ease of mind. Flinging a pile of wood on to the dying fire, he sought inspiration from the flames; but found none. There came instead poignant memories.

Memories of his wedding day five years ago, when it had teemed with rain, the best man had fumbled with the ring, and the reception had fallen flat. For all that, it had been the happiest day of his life, because fate, with all her tricks, had not taken Margaret away from him. But now, Margaret had taken herself away....

Gregory lost all count of time as he sat before the fire. He did not hear the car draw up outside the door half an hour later, or the turn of the key in the lock. He did not know that Margaret had come into the room until she switched on the light and spoke.

"Hello darling. I'm back! Hilda turned up after all and she's looking after Mother. As soon as Hilda came, I popped into Mr. Baxley's house to phone for a taxi. I had difficulty in getting a connection, because some idiot was trying to get through, but rang off."

Gregory said nothing. It was as though Margaret had appeared from the flames, conjured up in his dreams.

"You look as though you've seen a ghost," Margaret went on. "The taxi's outside, waiting to take us to the dance."

Gregory groped for words. "This… This note you left," he stammered. "What does it mean?"

Now it was Margaret's turn to be puzzled. "It means what it says, of course." She picked up the note; then burst into laughter. "You *are* a silly, darling. You should have turned the note over."

Gregory read the note again, and he read on both sides of the scrap of paper.

GONE TO MOTHER'S AS I SAID I WOULD
BUT THIS TIME I'M LEAVING
YOUR DINNER IN THE OVEN.

Elevenses at Lunchtime

Stretching his long legs lazily, Gerald felt on top of the world. He had been pinnacled to this Everest of emotion by the comfort of a first-class carriage (for which he was charging the firm) and the anticipation of a luncheon date at which he hoped to land a big deal. His mellow mood was further enhanced by a carriageful of cheerful faces.

As befitted a super-charged, high-powered salesman, Gerald liked to see friendly faces about him; too often his fellow travellers resembled a bunch of dyspeptic undertakers who had missed the treble chance by one point. But today, for some reason, a universal smile was directed at him....

Alighting at Cash-on-the-Nayle, he instructed the porter to send his suitcase to the Hotel Splendiferous. The case contained the latest collection of samples from head office—bait to catch one of the biggest fish in commercial waters. If Gerald landed the fish, he could look forward to a handsome commission and, probably, that vacant sales-managership.

Lunch was at one, which left him an hour to while away, in what seemed to be as one-horse a town as had ever disgraced a map. As it happened, however, the hour was to require no whiling whatsoever.

The fun started when Gerald bent down to tie his shoelace and was horrified to note that he was wearing odd shoes. Stylish shoes, granted; but odd. One black, one brown. Little wonder that people had been smiling at him in the carriage!

Now Gerald was a fastidious dresser, from the snappy trilby on his sleek black hair to the neat—and usually matching—shoes some six feet six inches below. Indeed, his sartorial elegance was the chief weapon in the armoury of his salesmanship. He simply must get another pair of shoes before meeting his client; otherwise he would lack the confidence to pull off the deal. Particularly as the commodity he had to sell was—footwear.

But there was a snag; he was not an off-the-peg dresser, and he took size 11 in shoes.

The first shop he called at was closed for lunch. The second one might as well have been too, for all the purpose it served. "Size 11?" said the assistant. "I'm afraid you'll have to wait a bit."

"I have precisely 55 minutes," said Gerald.

"Not quite long enough, sir. It'll take two weeks to get a pair that size."

Gerald didn't try a third shop, for there was no other shoe shop in town.

But the imagination and resource which had rocketed him supreme in the shoe sellers' sphere, stood him in good stead now. He stopped a small boy and asked: "Where does the biggest man in town live?"

Dismissing the lad's query—"Is it cold up there?"—as a thirst for unessential knowledge—Gerald strolled away to the address given. The woman who opened the door to him was as gigantic as Gerald hoped her husband would prove to be; she was Extra-O.S. in all departments.

"I want a pair of shoes..." he began.

"I want a pair of nylons myself," was the reply, "but I don't go knocking up strangers for 'em."

Here was surely a case for the exertion of his charms, and Gerald poured out his dilemma. "And a small boy directed me here," he concluded, "because he thought your husband might help."

The woman, who enjoyed the sense of humour usually associated with one of her bulk, replied, "And so he might help; he does take size elevens. Ah, here he comes." And as a half-pint, size-four-shoed midget appeared, she added: "Size 11 in collars, I mean!"

Gerald didn't think this at all funny. He consulted his watch anxiously; precious minutes were ticking away. "Who's got the biggest feet in town?" he asked desperately.

"My Ada," said the midget proudly.

Gerald glanced at the woman's feet wistfully, overcoming the urge to borrow her shoes. "But who's the biggest man?"

The woman, having enjoyed her fill of joking, relented. "I should say that Mr. Rymer might be able to help you, young man. He lives in the big house down the end of the lane."

Gerald machine-gunned his thanks, and shot off down the lane like a streak of lubricated lightning. But there was no answer to his knock on the end house door. 12:25. There was no time to stand on ceremony, so he shinned up a drainpipe, hoping to gain entry through an upstairs window.

"Stick 'em up!" bellowed a fruity voice suddenly from below.

Gerald stayed rigid, hoping to be mistaken for the drainpipe. But the fruity voice repeated its request, its owner backing up the invitation by prodding the protruding posterior with a shot gun.

Gerald put up his hands and thus releasing his grip on the drainpipe, slid ignominiously to the ground. He picked himself up ruefully and surveyed his captor. Mr. Rymer, like Gerald, was in his early thirties. He had a fruity face to match the voice—a cherry red complexion ripened by English country air and foreign country wines. A giant of a man with, Gerald was pleased to note, a size 11 foot.

Gerald's agile brain sought an excuse for house-breaking; but as it happened, in one sentence Rymer presented him with both alibi and an alias. "Bless my soul, Potty Parsloe!"

Gerald didn't relish this reflection upon his sanity, but anything was better than a charge of attempted burglary, and more important, the time-lag that went with it in proving his innocence. The mantle of Potty Parsloe having descended on him, he fitted it to his slim shoulders. "Hello Rymer old bean," he beamed fatuously. "I happened to be passing so I thought I'd—er—climb in."

Rymer chuckled. "Same old Potty. I see you're wearing odd shoes."

Gerald winced. "As a matter of fact, Rymer, I want to borrow a pair of yours. Two of the same colour."

"Two of the same colour! Come, come, Potty, you must be sane!" As he spoke, Rymer led the man who he firmly believed to be his old school chum into the house. Inside the study, he poured out the drinks. "What'll you have, Potty?"

"A pair of shoes, please," said Gerald, with one eye on the clock. "Size 11. Neat."

"A drink first," Rymer insisted, "and a chat over old times."

Gerald sat in an easy chair, uneasily, sipping vintage brandy and swapping vintage anecdotes. Never had he spoken with such assurance about characters he had never met, or re-lived so many scenes he had never appeared in. And if at times he was a little vague—well, wasn't that just like old Potty?

It was ten minutes to one before Gerald could persuade his host to provide a pair of shoes. And even then his worries weren't over. "If you're lunching at the Splendiferous at one o'clock," said Rymer, "you'll be lucky. It's right the other side of town."

Gerald groaned. "Then lead me to your telephone. Urgent!"

Rymer lifted his eyebrows. "There's a phone in the hall—but I didn't think you could tell the time, Potty."

Thanks to a succession of wrong numbers, it was well past one before Gerald got his connection. "Yes," rasped a voice at the other end of the line. "Mr. Finglehart speaking. Outrageous way to treat a businessman. I've already started on my lunch, but I'll see it's charged to your firm. Yessir, I'm a businessman, but I'm not putting any business your way."

Gerald held out a tentative olive branch.

"My samples are already at the hotel, sir. Perhaps you'd care to look at them until I get along?"

"H'm—well, that's different—we'll see," Finglehart snapped, and rang off.

At one-thirty Gerald bade his new-found old friend a fond farewell and made his way to the Hotel Splendiferous. Even if there was no order awaiting him, he had to pick up his case of samples. Entering the lounge, he spotted a dark-suited gentleman pacing the carpet. "Mr. Finglehart?" he asked apprehensively. "I'm awfully sorry...."

Finglehart cut him short. "Sorry, nothing. Here, take this!" He handed over an official looking document which Gerald read blankly: *Please supply: 100,000 pairs of shoes....*

"But I thought you were hopping mad at me," Gerald said, unable to disguise his relief.

His client smiled. "I *was* hopping mad. Literally hopping; my corns were giving me jip. Then after you rang me, I tried on a pair of shoes from your sample selection. They're marvellous, my boy. And was I relieved to find a pair that fitted me! You see, I take size elevens."

Escape to Death

The man who was a number slid through the pantry window. Stealthily he picked his way through the kitchen, the dining room and so into the lounge.

The occupant was reading his evening paper and did not look up until he heard his name spoken: "Maxley."

Tubby Maxley swivelled in his chair and regarded the intruder with a glance in which surprise and fear were equally blended. His newspaper fluttered to the floor. "Vanson!" he exclaimed.

Rex Vanson vaulted over the settee and sat down. Five years in prison had kept his figure lithe and trim. "I've come to keep my promise, Tubby," he said. "Remember?"

Because Tubby did remember all too well, he changed the subject. "I—I heard you lost your good conduct remission and were having to serve your full time."

A cat-and-mouse game suiting Vanson's mood, he pursued this line of conversation. "Your spies are well-informed, Maxley. I was due for release tomorrow, but yesterday I blotted my copybook It was naughty of me to throw a mug of cocoa into the warder's face; but it was calculated naughtiness. You see, *I didn't want to be released*!"

"Then what are you doing here?"

I told you, Tubby. I'm keeping my promise." Vanson reached for the packet of cigarettes on the occasional table beside him, and lit one. Maxley stretched out a podgy palm, expecting to be offered one of his own cigarettes, but the prisoner slipped the carton into his pocket.

Vanson was silent a while as he puffed away, thinking back to yesterday's cocoa-slinging episode. He had been sorry to treat the warder in this fashion, for Rivers had looked after him pretty well. The Governor, too, had been a tolerable cove, and he would have overlooked the incident had Vanson been prepared to apologise to the warder. But the affair had been calculated, and apology was not the answer to the calculation.

Maxley, having no soothing cigarette, knotted his tie. He brushed his sparse hair with a perspiring hand. He spluttered. He stammered. "If—if you have lost your good conduct remission, Vanson, how—how did you get here?"

"By the 8 p.m. fast train from Pennystone," the tormentor replied. "Highly recommended. Only a 20-minute run."

"Then you *were* released?"

"No, I escaped. It took me nearly four years to build that tunnel—only finished it today—and I was determined that when I came out I was to travel via the *Under-ground.*" Vanson chuckled at his own joke, but his host could only achieve a mirthless grin.

"You're crazy, Vanson. You could've walked out tomorrow, but for your violence."

"Violence, ah yes." Vanson seized on the keyword. "Violence. That brings me to business. Remember our last meeting?"

Maxley's bulk quivered. He had remembered little else for some time past. The scene was the Old Bailey five years ago. Now, his memory developed the mental negative and his fear enlarged it; Rex Vanson being led to the cells—a hard, bitter, forlorn figure. Suddenly, Vanson had turned, and shaking a fist in the direction of the man whose evidence had convicted him, shouted: "*When I come out, Maxley, you rat, I'll kill you.*"

Maxley didn't like the picture at all. He tried another conversational detour, along the path of Vanson's ego. It might yet lead to friendliness and safety. "Tell me about this tunnel, old man. Clever of you to get away with it."

Vanson smiled, lit another cigarette from the stub of the first and blew a smoke cloud under the nostrils of his narcotic-starved victim. "Oh, I wouldn't say clever. Not to one who had a bit of practice in Stalag V.20, and who had plenty of time on his hands.

"In one corner of my cell, I've got a heavy iron trunk containing some personal belongings. I made a trapdoor in the floor, about 15 inches square, for entry into the tunnel. The cut edges of the trap were barely visible, but in any case the trunk has been an excellent cover all the while.

"So into the tunnel, and out again at the other end, to a convenient scrub of common land well outside the prison gates.

"As for the tunnel itself, well, that represented month after month of patient graft; but of course I was spurred on all the time by the object of my escape—*to keep my courtroom promise.*"

Rex Vanson looked at his watch. "Well, this is no time for idle chatter; I have another appointment." He stood up. Maxley remained seated, petrified by the sudden glint in his visitor's eyes—a duplicate of that hate-ridden courtroom gaze.

The convict examined his hands and carefully brushed off the remaining traces of soil picked up in the tunnel. Then he made a sudden dart in Maxley's direction, and the lean brown hands were encircling the puffy neck. The fat man's screams were cut off at the main.

"You—you'll soon be back in jail," was all he managed to say. The words constituted his last gasp.

"I know I will," Vanson murmured. "I'm taking the tunnel back!"

That precisely had been his plan. When the police came to investigate Maxley's murder, as a free man Vanson would automatically be Suspect No. 1. Safe in jail, however, he would have the perfect alibi.

Leaving the house as he had entered it, Vanson hurried off to the railway station. Within half an hour he was in Pennystone, making towards the jail to locate his point of departure from the tunnel. There it was, conveniently close to a gorse bush, untouched during his brief absence.

He crawled down to the tunnel bed, and his first task was to seal off the exit. The tunnel must never be discovered, or *phut* went his alibi. He sealed the gap by pulling away the shoring boards; Nature assisted him, for the dislodgement of one board produced a miniature landslide. The earth was now comfortably banked up behind him, blacking out the moonlight above.

He grinned. Sealing-off the other end would not be so easy, he thought. It would take him time to fill in the crevices around the cell-floor trapdoor, hair-fine though they were. He might yet need to sacrifice a further good-conduct remission by throwing another mug of cocoa.

He crawled slowly along, purposefully, painfully. The going was tough; the atmosphere foetid; he found difficulty in breathing. About halfway along, a fall of earth impeded his passage, but he managed to wriggle through, his energy almost spent.

At last he was at the jail end of the tunnel, the freedom of prison directly above. Somehow, he couldn't help thinking about the cocoa, hoping that it wouldn't be necessary to repeat the attack on Rivers, who was such a decent sort....

So decent a sort was Rivers that at that moment he was inside Vanson's cell. An indulgent mood had taken him along there to persuade the prisoner to apologise.

Rivers saw a dummy in bed. The warden drew the wrong conclusion: Vanson must have escaped from an outside working party. He shrugged his shoulders. Had it not been for him, Rivers, the prisoner would be free tomorrow, anyway. What was a mug of cocoa between acquaintances? Let sleeping dummies lie!

The warder switched off the light. After he had done so, his knee bumped against an iron trunk; so Rivers shifted this some two feet along to its rightful place in the corner....

Below in the tunnel, Vanson was thumping on the weighted trap and shouting for help, until he had no breath left in his body.

Figment of the Imagination

"You can't see Mr. Barcroft, sir," said the maid. "Nobody does without an appointment."

"I think he'll see me," the visitor assured her with an easy charm. "Tell him that I too have business dealings with Mr. Stanley Wakenden."

Twenty seconds later, the visitor was stretching his legs on the settee in Barcroft's study, surveying his host's repellent (and momentarily puzzled) features.

"Well," Barcroft snapped, "who are you?"

The visitor smiled. "I'm allergic to proper names, so I'm here under the alias of Max."

"And what's the nature of your business?"

"My business, Barcroft? Pickpocket and blackmailer to the trade."

Max leaned back and lit a cigarette whilst that information set in. He was a nondescript individual of indeterminate age, who might have passed unobserved in any crowd. (Useful attributes in one whose profession is pickpocket.) Except that, perhaps unusually, he chose to sport an R.A.F. moustache and horn-rimmed glasses. Still, he knew his business best; as his next words testified.

"I picked your pockets earlier this evening, Barcroft."

"Why, you rat—" Barcroft half rose in his chair.

Max held up a slim, well-manicured hand. "Easy there, old chap, let me finish. It was while we were all playing boomps-a-daisy in the parked tube train. They might as well name the Piccadilly Line, the Pickpocket Line."

"Cut the gags," Barcroft snapped. "Give me back my wallet."

"So you've missed it, eh?" I bet you didn't report the loss to the police, even though ostensibly you are a respectable businessman."

"So I am indeed!"

"Oh? Well, a document in your wallet proves you also to be a blackmailer."

"Blackmailer. That's an ugly word, Max."

"You're an ugly man, Barcroft."

"What is this document in my wallet supposed to have contained?"

"A rough draft of a new blackmail contract you proposed to draw up with Stanley Wakenden. As if you weren't bleeding him enough, you intended to step up the charges."

Barcroft laughed, uneasily. "Why, I'm an author as well as a businessman. Stanley Wakenden is a figment of the imagination."

Max blew a casual smoke ring. "I saw you with this 'figment' an hour ago on your latest bloodsucking session, so I followed you on to the tube. I happen to be blackmailing Wakenden myself."

"What do you want me to do?"

"Lay off my client, Barcroft. His blood bank won't stand two leeches digging in."

"And how do I know you've really got something on Wakenden?" Barcroft asked suspiciously. "Maybe you're just a cheapjack trying to capitalise on a lucky pickpocket haul."

"Oh, no, I have the same sort of evidence as you, Barcroft, that Wakenden did a stretch in jail before he turned over a new leaf. See here—a letter that he once wrote with a prison address. And if either of us exposes him, it will ruin his business. He's paying good money to save that exposure."

Barcroft was impressed; but unmoved. "And supposing I don't withdraw from this lucrative business, my friend?"

"You *will* withdraw, Barcroft. I'm blackmailing you too…. Unless you hand over whatever hold you have on Wakenden, I will expose *you* as a blackmailer to the police. They'll be interested to see the contents of your wallet."

And then, with jaundiced eye, Barcroft suddenly saw his visitor as a whirl of arms. Max tore up the letter, threw it on the fire, and snatched off his horn-rimmed glasses and R.A.F. moustache.

"Good God—Stanley Wakenden!" Barcroft exclaimed.

The visitor turned at the door in farewell. "None other! Did I not say that I came here under an alias? Incidentally, the crime for which I once did a stretch in jail was pickpocketing."

Girl with a Dream

To Marian the telephone conversation seemed never-ending. The boss was doing his best to cut short the client at the other end, but the caller wouldn't take the hint. Like a rippling brook, the conversation went on and on. Soon Marian felt herself day-dreaming; and in accompaniment to her truant thoughts her pencil doodled across the pages of her shorthand notebook in deft, copybook strokes. And most un-businesslike strokes they were. She wrote of Springtime… and of Love.

Perhaps it was the brave shaft of early Spring sunshine, lighting up the musty office that led her thoughts in this direction. The advent of Spring never failed to re-kindle the spark of romance in her heart. But season followed season and now she was nearing 30, with the kindled spark yet to be fanned by fate into the flame of a live romance. Philosophically, she had always left the selection of a Mr. Right in the hands of fate, but at times like these she was apt to wonder just how capable those hands were.

At length young Mr. Redfern replaced the receiver, and he said; "Sorry about that, Miss Danecourt. Would you mind reading back from the beginning?"

Only half awakened from her reverie, Marian read:

"Dear Sirs—We have to acknowledge your letter of the 10th instant, and are surprised to note the attitude you adopt. Nevertheless… Spring has come and my heart—"

"Did I say that?" Mr. Redfern's tone of surprise jerked Marian back to reality; and a rose-pink blush tinged her cheeks, offsetting becomingly the mass of dark curls above. "I can't think what possessed me to write that," she apologised.

To cloak Marian's embarrassment, Mr. Redfern glanced at his watch with a well-feigned casualness, and exclaimed: "Good Heavens! It's lunch time. We'll have to leave that letter."

Gratefully, Marian rose to go, but as she reached the door the managing director called her back. "Would you care to accompany me to lunch, Miss Danecourt? Now that you're my private secretary we should get to know each other better, don't you think?"

In all her fifteen years' business experience Marian had not met a boss so pleasantly informal as Lawrence Redfern. Wilberforce Redfern had retired a week ago, handing over the reins of the office to his son; and the newcomer had been heralded by a splendid reputation. He was said to have made a study of psychology, applying its methods with good effect to every commercial relationship.

"Thank you, Mr. Redfern. I shall be pleased to come." Perhaps, Marian thought, the lunch date would help to relieve her heartache. Who knew? It might even provide the cure!

*　*　*　*　*　*

The little restaurant in the side street off the Strand was quiet and cosy; select without being ostentatious. It matched Mr. Redfern's personality, Marian felt; and it was the sort of place she would have chosen for herself had her purse strings allowed.

Despite the splendour of the surroundings, Marian did not look the least bit out of place. Following Redfern to their table, she walked erect with a mannequin-pose; and her well-tailored light grey suit and new Spring hat were as smart as any outfit in the restaurant, albeit Marian's wardrobe had sprung from less expensive fashion houses.

Tackling her roast chicken, Marian smiled to think of the packet of cheese sandwiches lying untasted in the office. By the time the coffee stage was reached she was sharing her smiles, and her thoughts, with Lawrence. She found herself speaking of her family life; of her hopes and fears, her aspirations and ambitions. Somehow, it did not seem at all strange talking like this to Mr. Redfern, for his magnetic personality—like that of a family doctor—invited confidence and confidences.

She told how her parents had been killed, leaving her at the age of twenty in sole charges of three young brothers. How she had been to the boys since that day father, mother, uncle and aunt all rolled into one.

She told how she had been courting at the time of her parents' death—walking out, to use the teenager term. How he had walked out; right out of her life. He hadn't fancied the prospect of the post of foster-brother-in-law to three growing lads.

Lawrence Redfern was a sympathetic listener as Marian poured out her story. This tall, slim woman had a dignity which suggested that she tackled her household problems with the same efficient manner with which she dealt those of the office. The cares of a double-length day had not trespassed on Marian's features. Her pretty, still-young face possessed a calm repose which worry and hard work could not eradicate—a repose which had been etched there by the hand of a sense of humour.

"How about current men friends?" Lawrence prompted.

Marian smiled. "Imagine," she replied. "Office work every day. Housework in the evenings. Shopping at weekends—"

"And at all odd times." Lawrence joined the chorus. "Laundering. Darning—"

"And mending."

"Trousers patched in triplicate?" Lawrence suggested.

Marian nodded. "Although, of course, my brothers have outgrown that stage now. But you can see I haven't had much time for Romeo-hunting. Still"—emphatically—"it's been great fun, and the boys have been worth every minute of it."

Lawrence lit up his pipe and took a few reflective puffs before commenting, in the manner of a judge summing up the evidence: "You know, Miss Danecourt, there's something of the fatalist in you. That is all right up to a point, but you shouldn't leave everything to chance. Find time to meet new friends. Give fate a gentle dig in the ribs."

As Marian shook her head doubtfully, Lawrence added: "Then we'll have to find a husband for you."

"Thank you, Mr. Cupid. I'll have a tall, dark, handsome man, bronzed of course with grey-blue eyes. Say about thirty-five."

The type Marian described was a sort of composite picture drawn from magazine illustrations, cinema heroes and men she had conjured up in her daydreams. (She couldn't place the type she had met in her "night" dreams, because the picture had always faded by morning.)

Even as she spoke, Marian realised with a shock that the description she gave fitted Lawrence Redfern in every detail. For the second time that day, Marian blushed; and for the second time Lawrence's watch came to the rescue. "Great Scot! It's a quarter past two. We should be getting back to the office."

* * * * * *

Back in the small office which she shared with Patricia Welmore, the head of the typing pool, Marian was greeted with a supercilious sneer. "You haven't lost much time lunching with the boss. Don't tell me you're in love at last."

Patricia was the date-a-night type, shallow and self-centred; a platinum blonde whose colouring owed more to the skill of the manufacturing chemists than to Nature. She was forever boasting of her conquests, and Marian had lost count of the times Patricia was alleged to have been engaged. It was significant that her engagement ring was the same with each new courtship, and that before going out in the evening she carefully transferred the ring from her second finger left hand to the second finger right. A jealous type, not to be trusted.

Marian ignored the cheap jibe, and sitting at her typewriter, was soon rattling away at the keys. Her work was mistake-proof that afternoon. Whilst she worked she pondered, and so her typing—as a subconscious effort—was perfect.

She thought mostly of Lawrence Redfern. Was he the Mr. Right whom fate had been keeping up her sleeves? Analysing her feelings, Marian was not so sure. Certainly, compared with her daydream lover, he might have been made to measure for the part. Equally surely, he was temperamentally ideal. A wise, kind, charming man.

But somehow there was no responsive voice from within which cried: "That's the man for you!"

At times like these Marian half-envied Patricia her worldly experience. Had she herself met half the types Patricia had, she might at least have been granted a clue. How else could she determine whether her liking for Lawrence was the real thing?

That question haunted her for the rest of the day. For the rest of the week. For a whole month.

* * * * * *

Sitting one evening in the darkened living room of her trim suburban villa home, a prey to her nimble mind, Marian did not hear her brother Peter come into the house. Did not hear his merry snatches of song as he executed a step dance in the hallway, seemingly unaware that it wanted but five minutes to midnight. Peter was not drunk—unless the Elixir of Love could be said to be intoxicating. He pranced into the room, turned on the light and leaped straight on to the settee. He came within an ace of crushing the life out of his sister.

"Gosh! Why have you been sitting in the dark?" was his bewildered greeting. "What's on your mind?"

Marian neatly sidestepped the question, countering with one of her own: "Why are you capering about at this hour?"

Peter chose one of a dozen phrases which sprang to his mind. "You'll soon have one less mouth to feed, Marian." Then, to underline his meaning: "Brenda says yes. We're going to announce the engagement officially on my 21st birthday next month."

"That's wonderful." Marian gave her brother a congratulatory kiss. "But why the gloom?" For a sudden idea, like the application of a damp cloth, had wiped the cheerful grin from Peter's frank, boyish face.

Peter handed his sister a cigarette and lit one for himself. "I do wish you would get married first," he said after a while. "It seemed only right that you should."

"Bless you, Peter. It needs two to make a contract, you know."

"What about this boss of yours? Nothing doing yet?"

"Nothing doing... ever. Even in the unlikely event of his asking me, I should have to refuse him. Mark you, that decision has no bearing on what happened at the office today."

"Tell me," Peter invited.

"This afternoon one of the young typists missed the pay-packet from her handbag," Marian explained. "She reported it to Patricia Welmore, who reported it to Mr. Redfern. Without more ado, he in turn reported it to the police. A plain-clothes detective sergeant turned up and interviewed us all in Mr. Redfern's office. At Patricia's suggestion, we all agreed to open up our handbags and.... Well, the pay-packet was in my handbag."

"Hard luck, old girl," Pater said. He took a deep puff of his cigarette, seeking from the large blue smoke rings words of consolation. "It was a plant, of course. That Patricia girl, I shouldn't wonder; jealous of your friendship with Redfern. But don't let that worry you."

"It doesn't worry me. The sergeant says the evidence is flimsy, and Lawrence thinks I'm innocent. My concern is at Lawrence's action in calling for the police so soon. Why, oh why, with all his human understanding did he do it?"

But the question remained unanswered that night.

*   *   *   *   *   *

The following morning was Marian's Saturday off. After a hectic round of shopping she was relaxing on a deck-chair in the garden when the front door bell rang. Michael, her youngest brother, went to answer the caller and after a few moments returned running into the garden: "Marian, there's a Mr. Wright for you."

Marian closed the library book she had been reading (a romance!) as Michael's words struck a chord in her imagination. She echoed: "A Mr. Right for me?" The illusion was but a fleeting one, however. "Oh, of course," she said. "Detective Sergeant Wright."

She went into the house to speak to the plain-clothes man; and his rugged countenance lit up in a beam of greeting, which stretched from one outsize ear to the other. "Thought I'd look in on you to put your mind at rest," he said. "After you'd left the office yesterday I had a further chat with Patricia Welmore. Faced with the threat of a fingerprint examination, she confessed to planting the pay envelope on to you.

"Mr. Redfern," the sergeant explained, "keen student of human nature that he is, suspected Miss Welmore all along, and he asked me to call at the office in a strictly unofficial capacity."

Marian smiled her relief and her thanks; an expression which the sergeant thought more eloquent than the fanciest of phrases. Some inner urge prompted Marian to invite the sergeant to stay to lunch, and he—having chosen the time of his visit carefully with this end in view—readily accepted.

The visitor got on famously with all the family and dropping the formalities at the outset insisted on being called Bob.

As Marian studied him covertly across the luncheon table, she had a feeling that they had met somewhere—long before their meeting at the office. But the sergeant didn't think so; although he said it was a pity they hadn't met sooner. And Marian found herself thinking along the same lines.

Bob was in no hurry to leave after lunch. Peter happened to be having trouble with his motor cycle; and Bob, donning a pair of overalls, was soon rendering strong-arm service flavoured with much useful technical advice.

Martin, the middle brother, had all the sixteen-year-old's passion for radio; and when the motor bike job was through Bob had perforce to rally round in the assembly of a homemade set.

Not to be outshone by his brothers, Michael, the fourteen-year-old, prevailed upon Bob to unravel a knotty point that had cropped up in his weekend school homework.

It was well into the evening before Bob left, and he departed armed with Marian's promise to accompany him to the forthcoming Police Ball.

* * * * * *

The dance hall was crowded. This was the first ball Marian had attended for many years, but she still retained her natural dancing ability. Bob had never had any dancing ability to retain. "As an ex-patrolman, I should be used to the beat," he quipped. "But I'm damned if I can follow this tempo."

"You're doing all right," Marian countered. *And so am I*, she told herself. For all Bob's clumsiness, she seemed to melt in his arms. And yet, Bob was not in the least like her daydream lover. He was tall, granted. Dark, yes. Handsome? The best that could be said about his features was that they were pleasantly plain. Nevertheless, conviction dawned within her; fate had at last produced a partner who would stay beside her long after the dance was ended.

As her heart accepted this truth, Marian realised in a flash where she had met Bob before. He was the hero of her dreams by night; his face was the face she had never been able to conjure up in the mornings.

They sat out in a moonlit corner of the terrace during the interval. "You know, Bob," Marian reflected. "Patricia did me a good turn when she played that trick on me. Otherwise I shouldn't have been enjoying this delightful evening."

"Oh, I don't know," Bob replied with a smile. "Lawrence Redfern was killing two birds with one stone when he sent for me that day. You see, I'm a very old friend of his, and if that incident hadn't happened Lawrence would have seized another opportunity to bring us together."

Marian's thoughts flew back to that luncheon date with Lawrence. "Find time to meet new friends," he had advised. "Give fate a dig in the ribs." She had shaken her head doubtfully at the time and so Lawrence, bless him, had done the rib-digging on her behalf.

Inside the dance hall the band had struck up again, but the M.C. found himself one couple short. At their table on the terrace, Bob had moved his chair closer to Marian. Placing a protective arm of the law about her waist, he said with an unnatural seriousness: "Marian, darling, I'm afraid I'll have to charge you with stealing."

Marian started, and Bob went on hastily, "With stealing my heart, I mean. For that crime I propose to take you in custody for the rest of your life, and your brothers with you, until they can act as their own custodians. It's my duty to warn you—I expect one answer only to the charge."

Marian snuggled up yet closer, and as she offered her lips to Bob she whispered, "It's a fair cop. I'll come quickly."

History Rehashed

King Harold of England was strolling along Hastings Pier for a morning constitutional. (He was, after all, a constitutional monarch.) Whiling away the time on ye pennye slot machines, he was joined by his equerry, the sharpest man in Hastings, whose name was B. Stings.

"How now, thou saucy varlet," quoth the king. "I really must get a pair of ye National Health glasses. I can hardly perceive what ye butler saw."

"Never mind that, sire. Methinks..."

"*Methinks*? Where's your grammar, lad? *I-thinks*."

Right you are, sire. I-thinks William of Normandy approaches the shores."

"What shores?"

"I'll have a double whisky," said the other quickly.

"Verily, thou malapert rogue," replied the king, "thou shouldn'test pull the royal leg; otherwise thou wilt sample the royal wrath in royal abundance, wist ye."

"If you're playing whist," said the equerry, "I'll go misere ouverte; that beats ye royal abundance."

The king changed the subject; partly because he was a man of action, and partly because he couldn't think of a witty rejoinder. "What preparations have been made to repel the invader?"

"None, sire. We haven't even rigged up a turnstile to admit them to the pier."

"Then summon me 10,000 yeomen, a brigade of boiling-lead squirters, and my prize panzer pea-shooting platoon. And incidentally, my quartermaster informs me that we have a fresh consignment of Bows from Harrow, and Arrows from Bow. Now where will I find the Archers?"

"On the BBC Light Programme, 6:45 every evening sire."

"I'll also want 10,000 scurvy knaves," the king continued.

"Thou art unlucky, sire. Since ye Court Barber introduced a lotion called Spillcream, every knave has been rid of dandruff. There isn't a scurvy 'un in the place Verily, thou hast had it, chum."

"Then bring me 10,000 saucy varlets in their stead."

"There's Ted?" said the equerry. "Where's Ted?"

"I told thee not to pull the royal leg," the king roared. He grabbed the jester by the scruff and flung him to the ground. Thus, the equerry was the first Englishman to be thrown out of the King's Arms whilst still sober.

"I warned thee thou wouldest not get away with it," said the king. And his victim fell heavily against a slot machine. But as he fell, a voice boomed put from the machine. "The weight of this wretched vagabond is thirteen stone ten." So he *did* get a weigh with it!

* * * * * *

The battle was not going well for Harold's men. Having invented the adage (wrongly attributed to Napoleon) that an army marches on its stomach, Harold had treated his troops to a three-course luncheon, commencing with pea soup. To make this, the cook had robbed the pea-shooter platoon of their ammunition.

Harold reviewed the situation with his equerry. "I'll have to call a truce," he decided. "Summon me a hot-foot messenger."

"I cannot, sire. The cowardly blighters have all got cold feet."

"Then I'll go meself," Harold quoth. So quothing, the king marched boldly up the hill to meet William.

William the Conqueror advanced with outstretched bow and arrow. "Have at you!" he challenged.

Harold advanced with an outstretched apple. "Have a chew!" he invited.

William took the fruit, nibbled at it, then flung the core back at Harold. It was a pippin (the shot, not the apple). It landed on Harold's eye.

"Woe is me," he moaned. "Alack-a-day."

"Keeps the doctor away," murmured his equerry, tactlessly. "Or am I thinking of an apple?"

"Woe is me," lamented the king. "With this eye injury, I shall never be able to see what the butler saw."

And with those last brave words on his lips, he kicked ye bucket.

Inside Information

When I entered the bar parlour of the Blue Boar, an Old-and-Mild at the corner table was holding forth on the subject of murders. I gather he set himself up as an authority on the strength of his having once queued up for ten hours outside the Old Bailey.

"Murder is easy," Old-and-Mild was saying, "despite what the detective stories tell you. In them, the criminals *have* to make the one vital mistake otherwise they wouldn't sell the books. But statistics prove that for every convicted murderer in real life, there are 751 unhung."

I could have corrected Old-and-Mild, but I let him have his say, for in all conscience the correct number was high enough.

"To say nothing," he went on, "of deaths by natural causes, which if the truth were known are very unnatural. Take young Bruce Robinson along o' the next village there, it makes you wonder, it does."

"But he were suffering from a rare disease!" protested Brown Ale.

"Ar," agreed Old-and-Mild, "murder is a rare disease."

Brown Ale wasn't standing for that. "But this were Butterkin's disease. Bruce told me. Invented by Dr. Butterkin in 1936."

"That's right," said a thin Stout. "Besides, young Dr. Thompson signed the certificate."

Old-and-Mild nodded. "He would, and very convenient too. Who's to say the doctor didn't kill 'im?"

I couldn't resist a comment here. "Be careful of the law of libel, old chap," I warned.

Old-and-Mild looked at me as though he knew I was a police inspector on holiday, and scoffed: "Huh! I know all about the law. This is a fair comment on a matter of public interest. Besides, I only said who's to say he *didn't* kill young Bruce."

"But why should he?" asked a Double Scotch, "and how could he?"

Old-and-Mild had the answers. "Who's to say he didn't prescribe poison in George's medicine? As to *why* he should, mebbe I've seen Dr. Thompson gallivanting about on the quiet with young Mrs. Bruce.

"Yes," he said, warming up to his subject—and throwing discretion to the winds in the process. "If Dr. Thompson didn't murder Bruce Robinson, my name's not Joe Wilson."

At this point the conversation was tactfully changed by the more moderate element in the far corner—a Shandy-drinking bloc; and I for my part dismissed the whole matter as idle local gossip.

A month later, however, an announcement in the local paper made me sit up. Just a few lines, but enough to send me scurrying to the telephone for a word in season with Headquarters: *The engagement is announced between Mary Robinson (widow of the late Bruce Robinson) and Dr. A. Thompson.*

They carried out an exhumation on poor old Bruce. It would be exaggerating to say that I expected them to find enough poison to exterminate a battalion; but I wasn't expecting the real diagnosis— Natural Causes, right enough—Dr. Butterkin's disease.

I got such a wigging from Headquarters for what they termed fishing for red herrings, that I decided to take it out on Old-and-Mild.

"Slander?" he chuckled, when I tackled him. "Defamation of character? Never. As a matter of fact, inspector, I knew you were a policeman and I was having a little joke at your expense."

"That's all very well," I reproved him, "but you went beyond the bounds of a joke when you said: 'If Dr. Thompson didn't murder Bruce Robinson, my name's not Joe Wilson.'"

Old-and-Mild laughed. "As a matter of fact, my name's Joe Smith."

Lady in Waiting

The waiting room at Little Mexford railway station was not a home-from-home at the best of times. Fogbound on a chilly evening, it was a dungeon.

That was Pamela Varnell's impression as she stepped into the waiting room from the draughty platform. A belt of fog followed her in.

The rays from a 60-watt bulb, suspended from the high ceiling, offered poor resistance to the murky invader. Pamela shuddered and chose the hard bench nearest to the fireplace—where a solitary ember bore mocking testimony to a blaze long since dead.

The whole setting struck a somber note to harmonise, in a minor key, with her current mood of cold, comfortless uncertainty.

The mood was born a month previously, when without warning David had ended their two-year engagement. Her shocked reaction was not one of injured pride, but the realisation that perhaps after all she had never really loved David anyway!

Fuel to her uncertainty had been added by the proposals of marriage from two colleagues at the bank where she worked. (They had a shrewd eye for a pretty brunette with brains, a sense of humour and a sense of proportion.)

Which of the two—if either—should she choose? A fogbound question, to be sure. Rapt in reverie, Pamela did not hear the waiting room door open, or see the tall, broad-shouldered man in the shabby raincoat (made for a smaller man) enter and slump on to the bench opposite to where she sat.

The first intimation she had was a breathless voice through the gloom. "I say, do you happen to have a cigarette? I'm dying for a smoke."

Pamela gasped at the sudden encounter. A less spirited girl would have screamed. She quickly recovered and took a cigarette case from her handbag. "Help yourself."

"Thanks, you're a life-saver." The stranger's voice was cool and cultured, if still a trifle breathless. "I assure you I am not in the habit of cadging cigarettes from ladies."

Pamela smiled; a bewitching smile wasted in the gloom. "If you would feel any happier about it, you can pay me for the cigarette."

"Willingly. But I haven't a sou, Miss er—"

"Then you make me out an I.O.U. The name is Pamela Varnell."

"I will, if you can supply me with a sheet of paper and lend me a pen. But first, have you a light?"

Pamela laughed. "You don't seem to be too well endowed with this world's goods!"

The stranger smiled ruefully. "No, but it's a long story, which I won't bother you with at the moment."

Pamela struck a match, and the flame enabled her to study the man opposite. Then she took a cigarette for herself and lit another match—to confirm her first impression.

She was attracted, and intrigued by what she saw. The stranger's face was pleasantly plain rather than handsome. He did not wear a hat, and his hair was ruffled as though he had been dragged through a bush. But the most striking feature was a large "black eye" rapidly turning purple.

Pamela scented a mystery. The mental exercise in trying to solve it dispelled the gloomy thoughts of her romantic dilemma. As an excuse to strike more matches, she took pen and notepaper from her handbag.

"This is for the I.O.U.," she said. "I'll light up again so that you can see to write."

Entering into the spirit of the occasion he wrote—"I promise to pay Miss Pamela Varnell the sum of 1.5 p. Signed, Lester March."

"Where do you live?" he asked.

Pamela did not reply immediately. She had just seen clearly beneath the stranger's dilapidated raincoat a uniform she recognised. A prisoner's grey overalls....

A train whistled in the distance, and a volley of fog detonators thundered a warning. Her emotions were now even more fogbound—although the romantic thread had been given a neat twist by this unexpected meeting.

She felt no less sympathetic towards the stranger because he was a prisoner—but should she help him to escape?

Lester March pulled the communication cord of her train of thought. "I asked where you live. I'll need to pay you back."

Pamela conjured a smile. "I live in Great Mexford, but you'll find me next week at Pennystone. That's ten miles up the line. I'm spending a winter week's holiday with an aunt who lives at Grey Gables."

"Grey Gables!" The remark was involuntary. "That's the big house opposite the prison, isn't it?"

Pamela nodded. Impulsively, she told Lester March why she was going there; how she planned to sort out the threads of a tangled love skein. So set was her purpose, she explained, she was travelling despite the fog—providing a train came.

"Will I see you at Grey Gables?" she asked artlessly.

There was no reply. Lester was groping in his pockets for a handkerchief. As he brought it out, a slip of paper fell to the floor.

Pamela picked it up. The light was improving sufficiently to enable her to read its message. "Contact Slippery Sid at 10 Green Street, Little Wexford."

She pretended not to have seen the incriminating address—which she guessed was a planned meeting place for the escaped prisoner. "You dropped this note," she said casually.

Lester took it and read it. "Thanks very much. I didn't realise I had that on me." He stood up suddenly. "Cheerio! I'll be seeing you." The door slammed and he was gone.

The next half-hour stretched into a minor eternity as Pamela weighed the pros and cons of two clear-cut courses of action. To tell, or not to tell? Clashing with her thoughts were the sounds of renewed activity on the railway as the fog gradually cleared.

This was not the sort of problem on which she could spend a week's holiday, as she could with her love-life problem. If she were to inform the police she must do so soon, otherwise the prisoner might get clear from the district.

It was that fact which finally swayed the balance. She rose with resolute suddenness, went to the telephone booth in the booking hall and dialled 999.

There was no sign of the train yet, and for the next half-hour she was a prey to misgivings. Her conscience was comfortably clear, but her emotions were in confusion.

At last came the rattle of signals and the apologetic puff of the overdue train. Dismally, Pamela picked up her suitcase and found an empty compartment.

As the train was preparing to pull out on the ten-mile journey to Pennystone, there was a last-minute scurry and a party boarded the end carriage. Among them were two policemen—and Lester March handcuffed to a prison officer.

Pamela did not know whether to laugh or cry. She did neither; she unburdened her feelings in a letter: *Dear Lester*, she wrote, *I hope you do not think too badly of me for turning informer. I'm sure in time you will realise it was all for the best. Don't forget, when you come out of prison I shall expect you to redeem that I.O.U.* She signed the note—*Lady in Waiting*.

When the train pulled in at Pennystone, Pamela stood near to the exit barrier and, as though by accident, bumped into the prison party. As she did so, she slipped the note into Lester's free hand. She gave the hand an affectionate squeeze. Then the gloom swallowed her up.

At Grey Gables, Aunt Matilda gave her a warm welcome. "Pamela, my dear, I didn't really expect you on such a night. Trust *you* to beat the fog! You can tell me all about it during supper."

But Pamela kept her thoughts to herself, and after supper insisted on washing up. While she was in the kitchen, the doorbell rang.

"I'll go, Aunt Matilda!" Pamela called out.

She was glad she did answer the bell, because on the doorstep stood Lester! He was now in civilian clothing. Hurriedly Pamela dragged him into the hall. Her emotions were a mixture of pleasure and alarm. "You fool!" she whispered. "You'll never get away with it again."

Lester laughed. "There's nothing to get away with. A prison officer is allowed to come and go as he pleases."

"P-p-prison officer?"

"The man you saw me handcuffed to, at the railway station, was the escaped prisoner."

Pamela was still bewildered. "But you were wearing prison grey, and he was wearing an officer's uniform."

Lester explained. "I had chased him ten miles across country before I met you. He had knocked me out and exchanged clothing. When I came round, I commandeered an old raincoat from a scarecrow and took up the chase again. I didn't know I had the hideout address in the prison trousers!"

Pamela's smile reflected sunshine after fog.

"I'm glad you telephoned the police," Lester said. "They helped me to arrest the prisoner at Slippery Sid's house. More importantly, a sense of civic duty will stand you in good stead as a prison officer's wife."

Lightning Conductor

Although the sun had long since set, the hunter found the heat oppressive. Weaving a hazardous path through dense foliage and prickly plants, he wiped perspiration beads from a sun-tanned brow.

"Lost!" he muttered. "I could do with a spot of light." But there was no light; moon and stars alike were coyly tucked up behind storm clouds.

The night was alive with the weird cries of the animal kingdom, and the darkness was intense. Scorched from the ravages of the midday sun, the hunter plodded on... and on. The delicate perfume of exotic blooms all about him held no fascination, but he would have given much for the whiff of pipe tobacco.

Relentlessly he groped a passage, the lure of the chase impelling him ever forward—with the urgency of the drug to the addict. In desperation he pulled out his torch again; but a mocking click confirmed that the battery had gone.

Then he remembered the matches. Swiftly he drew the box from his pocket, but in his excitement-palsied hands the match flared, flickered and failed. The second match was a dud. He did not strike another. He did not have another.

The hunter thought of his wife and children. They would be sitting down in comfort to supper just about now. He dismissed the thought and concentrated on his restricted progress as the inky blackness engulfed him.

Then—at that instant when the prospect was at its gloomiest—the storm clouds broke, and a lightning flash lit up the scene.

"Hurrah!" shouted the hunter. "I've got it!" He stretched out a grasping hand....

The whole exhausting day at Sandbank-on-Sea with the wife and kids had been one of self-reproach, for having left his favourite pipe behind.

Here, in the greenhouse.

Live Man's Shoes

Stanley Woodcott mounted the ladder of his career with easy strides, and at twenty-two was assistant manager in the firm of Jitterbug and Shufflebottom, mangle manufacturers. During the war he had taken the military rungs two at a time with the same agility, and rose to the rank of Regimental Sergeant-Major.

Then he was bitten by a bug. Not the common denizen of the army palliasse, but the more insidious Power Bug. As an R.S.M. Woodcott wielded his vast authority with grim relish and was voted the most unpopular individual this side of no man's land.

Upon de-mob, he was loath to lose this power, and it was only the prospect of a managership in his old firm which decided his return to Civvy Street. But back again as an assistant manager, now in his middle thirties, he had to mark time on the careeral ladder.

The post of manager was held by old Horatio Merryweather, who was still two years the right side of superannuation; and in that quarter Woodcott broke the Tenth Commandment. Granted, he did not covet Merryweather's ox, nor even his ass; but he did envy the other his exalted position. Not wishing to await a fitting of a dead man's shoes, Woodcott watched for the first sign of Merryweather slipping from the top rung, being prepared to apply a judicious downward shove.

An opportunity for such a shove arose when a rumour circulated the company that Mr. Merryweather was becoming an inefficient old dodderer—the symptoms being a return to second childhood. If only the rumour could be upheld, Woodcott intended to have a word in season with the directors.

He summoned the fountain head from which sprang most rumours in the firm, Alf Wyley, the garrulous office boy. There was no response to the buzzer. Remembering the adage about Mohammed going to the mountain, Woodcott swallowed his pride, and went along to the cubby-hole at the end of the corridor. He found the Fountain-Head of Rumour with his feet up, engrossed in his favourite bloodcurdler, *The Startler*. Woodcott's sudden entry startled the stripling more than anything in the thriller. He jumped to his feet in alarm, making a show of stamping letters that should have gone off the previous day.

With an effort, Woodcott addressed the lad genially. "Hello, young Scallywag. What's the magazine?"

The Startler. I happen to be reading it because Mr. Merryweather's only just returned it to me."

"You mean to say that Mr. Merryweather borrowed the magazine?"

"Pinched it. He said he was confiscating it 'cos I was reading in office hours. But akcherly—" Alf Wyley put on a conspiratorial air—"he wanted to read all about the marbles competition."

Woodcott was incredulous. "Why should the chief want to enter a boy's competition?"

"I heard him dictating a letter to Miss Smythe about it!" Alf exclaimed triumphantly.

"What's more," he added, "I live near Mr. Merryweather, and last Saturday I saw him coming out of a toyshop with a bowling hoop and stick. And the boss hates children!"

This news was far better than Woodcott had hoped to learn; he patted Alf on the back, promising for the first time in that youngster's recollection, to see that he got a raise.

Woodcott tackled Miss Smythe next; but she was less friendly than the office boy. "Mr. Merryweather did write about marbles," she said icily, "but it was a private letter." She tilted her pretty nose ceilingwards. "And I happen to be the manager's *private* secretary."

Despite the rebuff, Woodcott felt he was making progress. Miss Smythe had not denied Merryweather's interest in marbles. So Alf's bowling hoop story was probably also true. Woodcott next went into the heart of the enemy's camp; he invited his chief to lunch.

Now, at this period, business was brisk, and to celebrate the manufacture of the millionth mangle, the firm was holding a staff dance. Over the luncheon table, Woodcott broached the subject, artlessly. "Are you going in fancy dress, Mr. Merryweather?"

"The idea had appealed to me," was the reply. "I thought of going as a pirate chief. In contrast to my wife, who will be a crinolined lady."

"I can suggest a better contrast," Woodcott said cunningly. "Now there's some talk of you being too old for business. Why not confound the critics; prove that you are young still. Come as Peter Pan, a modern Peter Pan, say, with um… marbles and hoop and er… what have you."

Merryweather beamed broadly. "Thanks for the tip. I'll think it over."

Woodcott then had his first interview—the word in season with the directors. On the surface, of course, there was no reason why Mr. Merryweather shouldn't dress as he pleased at a fancy dress ball. Even so, it wasn't usual for executives to sport themselves in kindergarten fashion.

A week later the ball was in full swing, and no expense had been spared in its setting. The firm's canteen had been palatially decorated for the occasion, with potted palms, fountains and statues. Woodcott entered the building with anticipation, and he soon saw Mr. Merryweather, standing with his wife, inspecting the statuary lining the dance floor.

But Woodcott's face dropped as he noted that they had both kept to their original costume choice; he a pirate chief; she a crinolined lady.

Woodcott greeted Merryweather lamely. "Wot, no Peter Pan?"

Merryweather smiled knowingly. "No, but I did bring along those things you mentioned. I purchased the bowling hoop as a support for my wife's crinoline skirt. And the hooked end of the bowling stick makes an admirable artificial hand for my pirate chief, don't you think?

"By the way, Woodcott, d'you like these statues? I wrote to the organisers offering to loan them for the occasion. They're my collection of marbles…. Why, where are you going?"

Woodcott snarled. "I'm off to join the army."

Mean Time

It was a most uncomfortable elopement, Hector thought. Yet the time was right—the village clocks were striking midnight as the pair set off. And the setting was right—a romantic dash through the woods, short-cutting the route to the station.

But everything else was going wrong.

The suitcases weighed heavily on Hector's 50 years; though still paunch-less as a stripling of eighteen, his stamina only matched his middle age. The night was chill and a gale was whipping up, the bare-branched trees conducting raindrops down Hector's neck. As mud oozed into Hector's shoes, so romance oozed out of the situation.

Hector was essentially a romantic. His taste in literature leaned towards the novelette; for films he welcomed a dash of Charles Boyer. And now that he had come into a fortune, he could afford the "elopement" and still leave his wife comfortably provided for.

But practice was not living up to theory. The lush covers of a novelette, and the plush covers of a cinema seat, were considerably more romantic than the slush covers of this pot-holed path through the woods.

The girl 30 years his junior strode ahead, anxious to protect her hatless curls.

"Hold on, Mavis," Hector puffed. Peevishness distorted his good looks, emphasising the weak line of the chin, the petulance of the mouth. "I'm carrying the suitcases, you know." Remembering his film script, he added—"darling."

In reply, the girl pointed excitedly. "Oh, look! Shelter."

All thoughts of catching a train disappeared as Hector saw the dilapidated old manor house in the clearing; and sudden relief lent him the extra energy to sprint up the weed-infested drive.

A ground floor window, patch-worked with brown paper, afforded easy entry, and they were soon inside shaking off their wet coats. Hector tried the electric light switch, but a hollow click confirmed that the current had been disconnected. By the light of his torch he made out a few pieces of shabby furniture, and he led his companion to a creaky settee.

"A bit grim," he observed, "but at least at least it's dry."

He lapsed into silence as he sat down and retrieved his second wind with a generous measure of puffing and blowing. Suddenly the girl gasped, and Hector cautioned her to silence by a squeeze of the hand.

They were no longer alone; a mysterious figure carrying a lighted candle was making for a desk on the far side of the large room. Whether it was spectre or human they would not have been prepared to swear. The apparition wore an off-white nightshirt to colour-match a beard that camouflaged the face, and had a mass of hair that had seldom been introduced to a barber. He (if it *was* human) did not see the interlopers, having mind only for the writing pad on the desk on which he began to scribble. Then—"Confound it," he muttered, "it's gone."

And so within a few seconds had he. When it seemed unlikely that he would return, Hector went over to the desk and read by torchlight the cryptic message on the pad.

Six years ago, in a war-torn world.

Peeping over Hector's shoulder, the girl pleaded: "Let's get out of here. I'm scared."

But Hector's torch was roving the desk. "Hello, what's this?"

The spotlight played on a calendar. A cardboard calendar on which the whole twelve months were set out on the one surface. Nothing unusual about that... except that the year was 1924....

Hector had come across many stories where Time played tricks. It stood still; it skipped into the future; it flashed back; all at the whim of the author. But now it seemed the realm of fantasy had become a reality. If the calendar was any guide, he was living in the year 1924!

Six years ago, in a war-torn world, the night-shirted visitor had written. The reference could be to the 1914-18 war!

Hector was hardly aware of Mavis tugging at his sleeve. She pleaded again: "Let's get out of here. I'd rather face the gale."

He led her back to the settee. She was crying now. Absently, he patted her hand; and if there was any emotion in the act, it was a paternal gesture rather than a caress.

Whether or not he was suffering a delusion of Time; whether the apparition had been phantom or human; one factor was significant to the impressionable Hector. In roving the calendar, his torch had pin-pointed the central date of the year—Saturday, June 14th, 1924. His wedding day!

For long years past, he had shuttered the occasion from his memory. Now the wedding scene came battering at the doors. The simple service at the country church. The blushing bride with roses in her cheeks that owed nothing to cosmetics. The solemn words of the benign old vicar: "I now pronounce you man and wife."

How different from the contract he was now about to enter with the shallow, painted girl 30 years his junior. The only ceremony to be the handing over of a key by the hotel receptionist with the unspoken injunction: "I now pronounce you man and mistress."

Mavis nudged Hector out of his trance. "*Do* come along, dear. We'll miss our train."

"Right ho," Hector said briefly, "let's go."

The gale had subsided as the couple continued their journey in tense silence. At the station, Hector led the girl with gentle firmness to a taxi rank. "I'm sorry about this, Mavis, but I'm taking you home."

Seeming to sense the sanity of the situation, she allowed herself to be led into the cab. Hector stretched his limbs luxuriously. *No more lugging heavy suitcases*, he promised himself.

When the car pulled up at Mavis's house, Hector smuggled her back, in the same manner as she had left, then gave the cabby his own address.

As the taxi sped along, a reformed Hector, all bonhomie and benevolence, asked casually: "Know anything about a deserted house way back there in the woods?"

The cabby laughed. "Old Olivant lives there—the biggest miser since Silas Marner. Rakes in royalties from a best seller he once wrote; but won't spend a penny of it on himself or the house. And he's trying to write another to add to his hoard."

"I see." Hector was beginning to see the thing in perspective now. An eccentric author, inspiration-struck, comes down in the middle of the night, scribbles a few words; inspiration departs, and so does the author.

Then, if the apparition had been real enough, what of the freak of time?

Struck by an idea, Hector felt in his pocket for his diary, rapidly thumbing the pages to confirm his suspicion. Yes, his 1952 wedding anniversary fell on a Saturday. So! Old Olivant was so mean that rather than buy a 1952 calendar he used a 1924 edition, because the dates were the same!

Memo to Murder

"Memo: Must kill Hugo Crestock next time I see him," Jonathan wrote on his scribbling pad.

Jonathan Wepple had the world's worst memory. He should have been a professor, his witty friends were always telling him—or perhaps a plumber. But for 30 years he had jogged along as an accountant, shoring up a shaky memory with a memo pad.

It was Wepple's forgetfulness which had put him in Crestock's blackmailing clutches.

Because his colander memory had been developing more leaks— he was beginning to forget the most elementary items—he had been afraid he would lose his well-paid job.

Fear had led to blood pressure and a heart condition. So to cushion the threat of an early retirement, Wepple had swindled his firm out of £10,000.

But he had forgotten to make a double entry in the books which should have covered up the fraud, and Crestock—with his own eye to the main chance—had audited the accounts.

Though, as a middle-aged bachelor, Wepple was in comfortable circumstances, he couldn't go on buying Crestock's silence at £100 a month. Nor could he allow the blackmailer to go to the police.

So it had to be murder; and he was clever enough to get away with it, so long as his memory didn't let him down.

Out came the memo pad. "Plan for the murder of Hugo Crestock," he wrote.

"Medium: Poison—six of my heart tablets, taken at one go, will kill within a couple of hours.

"Time: Next pay-out day. Place: The curtained alcove of the Acacia Restaurant.

"Method: Crestock orders two beers, as usual, which will be served on a circular tray. I produce the money from my brief case; and while he is counting it, I slip the crushed tablets into the glass in front of me. Froth will camouflage the powder.

"Then, casually, I swivel the tray round, so that the drugged beer is in front of Crestock.

"He usually drinks up quickly and leaves immediately—and this will leave me free to wipe fingerprints from the glasses and tray. Well away from the scene, I destroy my dark glasses and false beard."

Wepple's sly grin changed to a frightened frown as he made a thoughtful footnote: "Remember to remove all clues." Then, so as to leave nothing to chance, he made another note: "Remember to destroy this memo pad."

On the next pay-out day—one to which for the first time he was really looking forward—Wepple stuck on the crêpe hair beard and put on the dark glasses which he always wore for this arrangement and set out for the restaurant.

But, so bad was his memory getting, he had to go home for the tablets which he had forgotten. Never mind—he took the chance of having another look at the memo pad, which of course he could not open in the restaurant.

Apart from that false start, nothing happened to sabotage the plan. The customary curtained alcove of the Arcadia was available. Crestock, the tall, young, icy charmer, greeted the sly, meek, middle-aged man with cold courtesy and counted the money carefully.

Then, a hundred pounds the richer, he drank his beer without suspicion and did not stop for social chat. Wepple was free to remove all clues.

And with the same sense of freedom he went to bed that night with an easy mind—the blackmailer out of his life for good.

But after a while there was an intermittent jabbing in the pincushion of Wepple's subconscious. Something was wrong.

Had he forgotten to remove any clues? No, on the whole he had managed pretty well without his memo pad actually in front of him. And the pad itself was now a mass of ashes. Fingerprints? Disguise? All taken care of.

Still he wasn't satisfied. "Wepple, old chap," nagged his subconscious, "you've had it." But if his subconscious was right, what was wrong?

Agitated though he was, sleep came before the answer did. It was a deep sleep… a very deep sleep.

Jonathan Wepple had the world's worst memory. He had remembered to drug the beer, but he had forgotten to swivel the tray round.

Old Joe Comes Up to the Test

Carchester Silver Prize Band had not won a prize (silver or otherwise) since 1913. That was the year Ben Filbey, the founder-conductor, had retired. Then the First World War took its toll and when the band was re-formed in 1920 the standard was several degrees lower.

As a combination to lead a carnival procession or to play a rousing march at the local football ground, the band served society well enough. But the connoisseur was not so easily satisfied.

Over the years bandmasters had come and gone; batons changed hands with relay-race regularity. Now at last, 55 years and one war later, a prize was once more within the band's grasp. Jack Ryland, an ex-military bandmaster, brought with him a new wave of enthusiasm, an experienced touch, and a half-dozen of his ex-army bandsmen.

Concert engagements followed and carnival organisers had to book months in advance, Carchester residents spoke of their band with genuine pride—the "melody-murderers" tag was discreetly dropped.

A signpost to success was set up by Bandmaster Ryland at rehearsal one evening. "Gentlemen," he said, "on my advice your committee recommend that we enter the Inter-counties brass band contest."

Awed gasps and gratified smiles greeted the news. If Mr. Ryland thought they stood a chance of wresting the coveted trophy from the best bands in the region, why should they quarrel with the recommendation?

The prospect of winning the contest meant not only a blaze of glory, but a round of public concert engagements. But to old Joe Filbey it meant simply a 50-year-old dream come true. When the bandmaster's announcement had settled in 39 musical (but mercenary) minds, a less agreeable thought arose. How could they think of contesting with old Joe on the euphonium? Poor Joe Filbey, on the wrong side of 70, was the sole link with the silver-prize-winning days. Ironically, he was also the main stumbling block to winning another.

Son of Ben Filbey, the founder, old Joe was a musician to his fingertips. Unfortunately, those fingertips were gnarled with arthritis and lost their way on several quaver runs. And breath came in jagged bursts, making his passages ill-phrased, and his tone....

Old Joe was the friendly butt of his fellow bandsmen, who respected his enthusiasm but were too young to recall his glorious heyday. Originally a solo cornet player, with the passing of the years and the passing of his natural teeth he had switched to a larger instrument. His walrus moustache framed the euphonium mouthpiece more symmetrically than the cornet, and this instrument also suited his rotund figure.

The band was entered for the contest, and excitement mounted when the test piece was produced at rehearsals. But after a preliminary run-through, fears of failure, founded on the presence of old Joe, were intensified. The euphonium was featured in several passages where the cornets (who might have camouflaged some of the mistakes) were given long stretches of rest. It was virtually a euphonium concerto.

When the bandmaster took Joe to task for a glaring error the old stalwart replied, "Don't worry Jack lad, it will come right in time. I've brought a tin of Limbo, the Lissom Liniment. It will smarten up me fingers.

"But seeing as you have stopped, Mr. Ryland, I might point out that in the second movement—where the euphoniums take up the melody—the trombones will have to play a little softer."

Ryland, who resented being called "Jack lad" and disliked even more receiving criticism from this quarter, replied with military sarcasm, "Perhaps *you* would like to conduct, Mr. Filbey."

"Yes!" said Joe, for that was his dearest ambition. If only he could take the band through just one number before he retired, he would be a happier man; following in the footsteps of his dear old dad. From time to time Joe had applied for the post of bandmaster, but the committee—whose only experience of his musical ability was at the receiving end of a euphonium—had always over-ruled.

Old Joe stood up now to take Ryland at his word, and the bandmaster said hastily, "Some other time, perhaps. Now we will take the euphonium passages again and the trombones can play as loud as they see fit."

After that episode there was much lobbying in committee to dismiss old Joe from the band. The constitution of the organisation was studied (after a lengthy search to determine that such a document actually existed), and legal loopholes were ferreted. To no avail. There was no provision for a retiring age or dismissal for inefficiency; no question of periodic auditions or refresher courses. There was no loophole at all, short of altering the rules; but here the lobbyists met with a sentimental bloc who wanted to retain old Joe for old times' sake. They were not averse to persuading him by friendly means, but the stubborn old warrior would not take the hint. He resisted suggestions that he should be appointed a non-playing librarian or that he should go on the mace.

The mace idea came from Sam Parker, a fellow euphoniumist who was particularly persistent in his persuasions. The strain was beginning to tell on Sam, who had to play more loudly to drown his comrade's cacophonies, to the detriment of his own exquisite tone.

Sam explained that he meant that Joe should carry the mace at carnival processions and parades. "You've no need to throw it much," he said. "Just hold it dignified-like."

Dignified-like, Joe replied that he was a euphonium player—not a comic caber tosser.

As the day of the contest drew nearer, so the hopes of the bandsmen receded. Limbo the Lissom Liniment failed to work the wonders forecast on the label, while Anno Domini continued to work its own brand of wonder.

* * * * * *

The eleventh-hour reprieve was as unexpected as it was welcome. At the bandmaster's prompting, the committee ordered a new set of uniforms for the contest; and when Joe saw the garish patterns of scarlet and gold he refused to submit his 50-inch waist to the tape measure.

"I'm not dressing up like a turkey cock," he declared. "The plain grey uniform designed by my dad is good enough for me."

"You must all dress the same," Ryland pointed out patiently. "As an old campaigner you should know that."

"I'm not putting on those fal-de-lals," Joe insisted. "So it seems I shall have to retire now—instead of next year like I planned."

They gave Joe a handsome farewell present—after all, such discord as existed was confined solely to his playing—and they went to the contest with renewed spirit.

Several coaches set out from Carchester on the big day. There was mild alarm when the bandsmen waiting to board the leading coach saw Joe approach the boarding point; for instead of his Sunday-best suit, he was wearing his plain grey, dad-designed uniform.

The alarm subsided somewhat when they noticed that the veteran was not carrying an instrument, and he was content to board one of the supporting coaches.

Burlingford Town Hall was crowded, but the organisers found a prominent seat near the front for Joe. He followed the proceedings with interest—tapping his foot here, jerking his palm there (as if conducting) and applauding the dozen smart bands who gave of their best to the test piece.

Carchester Silver Prize Band, brilliant in their Joe-less state, gave of their very best. They won the challenge cup.

When the cheers had died down the chairman, Alderman G. V. Lesvick, O.B.E., J.P., announced: "Now for the highlight of the festival. In accordance with time-honoured tradition the winning band will play the test piece again, as an exhibition."

More cheers. More anticipation.

"For this exhibition, again in accordance with custom, the composer of the test piece will conduct the band. And in this instance the composer has written under a nom-de-plume."

All heads were turned in the direction of Joe Filbey as he strode to the platform—a proud figure in the plain uniform designed by his father.

Joe took up the baton, tapped the music stand smartly and said, "Right, gentlemen. You did very well. But this time, perhaps you can all play the piece as I wrote it. In the second movement I want the trombones to play a little softer."

Oldest Inhabitant Dies

When I chose a cosy corner seat in the bar parlour of the Green Dragon, there was just one other occupant talking to the landlord.

He spotted me, and although bent by the weight of (at a guess) some 90 years, he hobbled in my direction with an alacrity that spelled a drink at my expense.

"Mild weather for the time of the year," he volunteered as he chose a seat at my table.

"Yes," I agreed. "It is mild."

The ancient applied an equally ancient ear-trumpet which he "plugged in" beneath bushy whiskers.

"Whassatt, you say?"

"Mild," I repeated.

"Thank 'ee kindly, zurr, I *will* have a pint of mild."

I gave the order, and resigned myself to the ordeal—but not without a struggle.

"It's a pity you haven't anything better to occupy your time with than to cadge free drinks," I reproved him.

"Cadge!" he spluttered.... "Your very good health, zurr. Cadge! Why, I'm the official village yarn-spinner, Oldest Inhabitant of Little Wychley, bar none."

He filled a clay pipe and ruminated as the noxious mixture permeated the bar parlour. "I might tell you, zurr," he hissed between jaundiced teeth, "Oldest Inhabitant-ing is a dangerous occupation. A matter of life and death. Arr, I could tell you a mighty interesting yarn about that."

"I'll buy it," I said... and bought two more drinks.

"30 year ago," said the ancient, "or mebbe 40, old Josh Marvin held the title of Oldest Inhabitant. 94 he were. He would have lived to be 100 if it weren't for the green door.

"He were leaning against the door—the door of this very pub— waiting for midday opening time. He were waiting to meet the red-headed stranger what he had spoken to the previous day."

I butted in. "Waiting for more free drinks, was he?"

"Not at all, zurr. Leastways, not entirely. He also wanted a bit more information, which he reckoned old Ginger-nob could tell him, to make the basis of an interesting yarn like.

"Well, there was old Josh at 12 o'clock. The sun was shining, birds was squawking and not a soul in sight. The clock struck the hour and the green door opened.

"At 2 minutes past 12, a shot rang out and poor old Josh dropped dead.

"At 20 minutes past 12, Police Sergeant Robins turned up— having just been called—a sharp one he were, for all his 15 stone.

"He asked Griggs what he knew about the murder.

"Griggs knew nothing. Or so he said.

"Then Sergeant Robins spotted old Bart Jacobs sitting at the bar as cool as you please, waiting to order a drink. Unpleasant character, he were, 92 if he were a day, and not a hair on his head, glassy eyes, and a beak on him that reminded you of a vulture. And that's what he seemed to be, with poor old Josh's body lying behind the bar there, covered up with a blanket.

"Sergeant asks old Bart what he's doing there and what he knows about the murder.

"'Nothing,' he says, dignified-like. 'And kindly remember, sergeant, I am the Oldest Inhabitant Presumptive. And now that old Josh is dead, I takes the title.'

"Griggs the landlord suddenly joins in the conversation. 'Exactly, sergeant. Bart's the only man in the village with a motive to murder old Josh. Josh didn't have an enemy in the world. Now he's gone, Bart steps in as chief yarn-spinner, and all the perks that goes with it.'

"That shook the sergeant, and he told Bart he had better accompany him to the station.

"Old Bart protested he was innocent. He had only been at the Green Dragon since 10 past 12, he said. In fact it was him who told the landlord to call the police. Griggs had done nothing up to 10 past

12, and in fact, Bart said, the landlord had been packing a suitcase to make a getaway.

"The sergeant then asked Bart what motive the landlord could possibly have for murdering Josh. So Bart told the sergeant *his* theory. Old Josh was a great yarn spinner, and the previous day a red-headed man had been talking to him, and he (Bart) overheard mention of the landlord's name. Perhaps the landlord had a guilty secret connected with old Ginger-nob and was afraid old Josh would split.

"That set the sergeant thinking again. So he ups and takes both Griggs and Bart to the police station."

The ancient paused in his tale to survey an empty glass. So I ordered two more mild ales.

"Which one did it?" I asked at length. "Griggs or Bart?"

The ancient chuckled. "That's what the whole village was asking. They was even taking bets on it. I backed old Bart at six-to-four, because he were favourite. Favourite to have done the murder, that is—being an unfavourite sort of character."

He shook his head ruefully. "I lost me money. Bart wasn't the one."

"What was the landlord's guilty secret?" I asked the ancient.

"Seems that ten years prior to the time I'm speaking of, Griggs and Ginger-nob done a robbery with violence. Ginger-nob gets caught and does ten years in prison. The landlord gets off scot free, changes his name and buys this pub.

"Well, when Ginger-nob comes out of clink, he hunts up Griggs. After finding him at the Green Dragon, he lays in wait the next day with a gun. The reason the landlord packed a suitcase to make a getaway was because he was afraid Ginger-nob would come back to kill him.

"Griggs opens up at 12 o'clock but suddenly sees Ginger-nob. And he slams the door shut again. Poor old Josh is ready to step in the pub; instead he steps into a bullet."

On Account of the Mice

The school master stood at the crossroads—in both senses of the phrase.

In the literal sense it did not matter which route Gregory Marvin took, seeing he was out for an afternoon stroll. But figuratively the decision he had to make would affect his whole future.

There was a bench at the crossroads, and Gregory sat down to seek in relaxation the inspiration he had not found in walking. A week had elapsed since Dr. Wickerby had delivered the ultimatum, but Gregory still suffered the shock.

On the eve of the brief half-term holiday the head master had summoned him to the study. "Mr. Marvin," the Head had said in his direct, forceful manner, "you are an excellent teacher."

"Thank you, Dr. Wickerby."

"And an asset to Crestleigh College."

"Thank you, sir."

"It doesn't follow, however, that you will make an ideal son-in-law."

Gregory had been lost for a reply. He had felt the same numbing sensation as the time he stopped a cricket ball with his forehead.

"In fact, Mr. Marvin, I forbid you to marry my daughter!"

What peculiar motive had activated the old man? Gregory had always got on well with the head master—as tolerably as one could get on with an autocrat.

"Admittedly, sir," Gregory had said slowly. "I took your approval for granted. But as Jean is of age, the question of permission doesn't apply. I shall marry her, of course."

"Very well, Marvin, you will be dismissed your post. I may remind you that I happen to own the school. The choice is yours, and I shall expect your decision at the close of the vacation."

"But what is your objection, sir?"

"Mr. Marvin, my motives may at times be peculiar, but I do not recognise the need to explain them to subordinates. Now go sir, and report to me a week hence."

Gregory sat by the crossroads. Zero hour was fast approaching. Sunshine lit up the country scene with friendly warmth, but it served only to throw into sharp relief the darkness of his tortured mind.

He thought again of Jean Wickerby. A charming, intelligent girl who shared his interest in school affairs. The girl he loved, genuinely if not perhaps passionately. Could he give up such a perfect mate?

On the other hand, could he give up the school with which he had been associated, as scholar and master, for 25 years? He had an affection for every grey stone of the college, every cloistered quadrangle.

It was all very well for Wickerby to deliver his illogical ultimatum; the head master was already married. True, Mrs. Wickerby was in delicate health; nevertheless they were a happy couple. It was unfair of the Head to take advantage of his ownership of Crestleigh.

No! He would not leave the college. So that meant... giving up Jean. A thousand pities, but the only choice.

Having made his decision, Gregory was about to go when a boy wearing a Crestleigh cap joined him on the bench.

"Hello, Mr. Marvin. Why aren't you home for the holiday?"

Home? The school was his home. The school was his life....

"Hello, Johnson Minor," he countered. "Why aren't *you* at home?"

The lad looked up, an earnest expression on his cherubic features. "Well, sir, it's on account of the mice."

"The mice?"

"Yes, sir. You see, my people are abroad so I can't go home, sir. I could have stayed with my Aunt Martha in Hampshire, sir, but I had to turn it down."

"Don't you like Aunt Martha's house?"

"Oh yes, sir. It's amazing!" Johnson Minor waxed eloquent. "It's got secret passages, a gun room, a haunted corridor, and a colour television set."

"Then why not go there?"

"Aunt Martha is scared of mice, sir, and I couldn't leave them behind."

The lad brought out a tattered wooden box and proudly displayed a pair of dingy white mice. "Meet Mickey Major and Mickey Minor, sir. I always carry them about."

Gregory was incredulous. "D'you mean to say you sacrificed a—a smashing holiday for the sake of these grubby specimens?"

The lad was plainly hurt. "Animals aren't specimens, sir. To me they're like people. And I reckon it's worth giving up things you like for the sake of people you like. Don't you, sir?"

There was a long pause.

"Don't you, sir?" the lad repeated.

"Ye-e-es," Gregory said. "Yes, perhaps you're right, Johnson. Well, I must be off now. I'm glad you came along."

He waved a cheery farewell to the boy, and with determined tread made his way back to the school.

The head master was pacing his study when Gregory rapped on the door. Dr. Wickerby would have been loath to admit that he had never been more agitated, but such was his state of mind.

As soon as the younger man entered, the head snapped: "Have you made your irrevocable decision, Marvin?"

"Yes sir." Gregory had never felt more certain of anything. "I shall marry Jean."

"Then you are dismissed your post."

"Very well, but I shall still marry your daughter. You might say, Dr. Wickerby, it is on account of the mice."

Gregory turned towards the door.

"Wait!" The head master stopped pacing and sat at the desk, motioning Gregory to do the same.

Dr. Wickerby's face was set in hard, anxious lines and he looked suddenly very old.

"It might interest you to know, Marvin, I too am faced with a problem admitting two clear-cut alternatives. My wife, as you know, is in delicate health. Now the doctors have ordered her to stay in

Switzerland indefinitely. Naturally, I should like to accompany her, but it will mean leaving the school to which I have devoted my life. For the first time in my experience I couldn't come to a decision.

"As you might imagine, Mr. Marvin, it is not my habit to seek advice. So I left the choice in the hands of fate.

"You, Marvin, are the instrument of fate. I set you a parallel problem and decided to follow the course you chose.

"You have put the love of a woman before the love of school, and I shall do the same. I shall now take up residence abroad."

Gregory whistled. "So you've blighted my future for the sake of a decision!"

Dr. Wickerby forced a wintry smile. "It so happens your future is not blighted, Mr. Marvin. You are more fortunate than I am. I shall always maintain an interest in Crestleigh College, and because you are now without a post, I am offering you the vacant position of Head Master."

Perfect Strangers

While balloons popped, Brenda sat quietly in a corner of the lounge, still sipping her first cocktail of the evening. All about her was the hubbub of a jolly suburban party—glasses clinking, voices raised in merriment. But in her present mood Brenda would have no part of it.

The Life-and-soul-of-the-party suspended an apple on a string from the ceiling and said with a cocktail-charged grin: "Roll up, me lucky lads and lasses. If you don't bite the bally old pippin first go, you pay a forfeit!"

Brenda wasn't amused. Parties without Graham weren't fun any longer. He had broken too many dates recently, pleading urgent private business. But what business could so urgently engage a sales ledger clerk? What affair was too private for a man to discuss with his fiancée?

She could find no answer to her questions, and only depressed herself still further in the asking. So with a synthetic giggle, she stood up to join the queue for the apple-bobbing game.

Life-and-soul-of-the-party doled out the forfeits.... "Brenda Marshmont, you will sally forth into the night with Cecil Lancaster. You each have to knock on the house of a perfect stranger and invite him (and her) to the party. Off you go!"

Twenty assorted bright young things accompanied Brenda and Cecil to the gate for a rousing send-off. Brenda waved an airy farewell, but unlike Cecil, she was too sober to knock on strangers' doors at midnight. She had a more sober idea. To call on Graham, and drag him back to the party! His parents were away on holiday, so there was no need for raised eyebrows at such a late call.

"Losing" Cecil was easy. She left him hugging a lamp-post, inviting it to a smashing party!

A wrap thrown loosely about her party dress, Brenda hurried on to Graham's house; her high-heeled shoes clicked a tempo to the accelerated beat of her heart.

When she reached the house, she was dismayed to find the hall in darkness. That meant either Graham was out or had gone to bed. In her present mood, Brenda scorned convention; she pressed the doorbell.

No answer.

She was about to turn away, when an instinct restrained her. A little guiltily she stooped and peered through the letterbox. Now she saw a glimmer of light filtering below the sitting-room door at the end of the passage. She pressed the bell again, with urgent impatience.

The next few seconds were action-packed. The hall light was switched on, the door opened, she was hustled inside, the door closed and the hall light switched off again. Graham's pleasant features were overcast. Perspiration oozed from beneath a thick mane of fair, tousled hair.

"Brenda!" he gasped. "Am I glad to see you!"

"Who were you expecting?" she asked coldly. "Another girlfriend?"

"No. The cops."

"Oh!" Brenda was shocked. She had come to "knock up" a perfect stranger, and it seemed Graham answered the description.

Shock turned to relief. At least there was no other girlfriend. Her happiness was not to be lacerated by the sharp edges of the eternal triangle.

Relief, in turn, changed to alarm. Graham was in trouble, and he needed her help.

He led the way into the sitting-room and slumped into an armchair. Brenda walked through to the adjoining kitchen and switched on the cooker. "I'll make some coffee," she said, "while you tell me all about it."

"I'm afraid this is a confession," he began ruefully.

Brenda said nothing, busying herself with the coffee cups.

"You see, darling, for the past two weeks I've been keeping an eye on Hulstone Lodge."

"Mr. Swanley's place?"

Graham nodded. "Rex Swanley is a rich young man-about-suburbia, fond of good living and good-looking girls. That's the whole point. He buys trinkets for all his lady-friends, and a trinket to Rex Swanley is a small fortune to me. He's out every night until after midnight, leaving his valuables carelessly about the place. Tonight I cashed in on his carelessness.... Look!"

He flung on to the table a pearl necklace, which glistened under the bright electric light. A thing of beauty, but not now (for Graham) a joy forever. He went on: "I was about to hide it when the doorbell rang. I thought you were the police."

"Why? Did they see you breaking into Hulstone Lodge?"

"No, darling. I got clean away before I bumped into Constable Dawson. Perhaps he didn't even recognise me in the dark, but like a fool I panicked and ran off."

"Was the necklace for me?" Brenda asked.

"Well, er, no," Graham replied. Then—as Brenda's face clouded over, her doubts swarming back—he went on: "Don't worry, sweetheart, it wasn't for any other girl, either. It was intended to pay for an early wedding. I simply couldn't wait another year."

"You *are* an idiot, Graham. I'd rather wait one year to marry, than wait five years for you to come out of jail."

"You're right, darling. I'm an impulsive idiot."

There was a sudden hissing sound, and Graham started. Brenda said calmly, "Now the milk has boiled over. But there's no time for coffee. You're coming back with me to the party."

She explained to the mystified Graham. "You need an alibi, and I can give you one. Everybody at the party is so deliriously canned, they won't know you haven't been there all evening!"

"And the necklace?"

"I've got the ideal hiding place."

With growing wonder, Graham watched her place the string of pearls around her neck, where they blended admirably with her neat party dress and suited her dark beauty.

"We're not likely to meet Rex Swanley," she said. "And even if Constable Dawson spots me wearing it, he won't suspect anything, because he won't know yet that a necklace is missing."

Hope gradually dawning within him, Graham accompanied Brenda safely through back streets to the house of the party. Festivities were in full swing, the lounge floor reverberating to the strains of Knees Up, Mother Brown.

Still in command, Brenda said, "You climb through the window, Graham, and merge with the throng. I'll join you later. I'm going to look for Cecil Lancaster; I left him clinging to a lamp-post!"

With his champion gone, Graham felt alone and depressed. He was only just beginning to realise how much he depended on Brenda. How he had neglected her in the past. How desperately he loved her, for her sympathy and common sense, no less than for her beauty. Supposing the police were to catch up on him? The thought of separation was more than he could bear.

Then, impulsively, he squared his broad shoulders. Brenda had shown him a way out—or, at least, a way in! She had told him to break into this crazy party. He opened a window, and thrust a leg over the sill. Soon he was one of the crowd....

A stranger grabbed him, in the manner of a lifelong buddy, and inveigled him into a game of Sardines. The rules were simple. You squeezed into a cupboard on the upstairs landing with about a dozen others. He really was like a sardine, Graham mused. Packed in by a whirl of events, unsure whether there was a way out....

Ten minutes later the cupboard creaked in protest and the mass of flying legs and arms was propelled downstairs. Graham jumped to his feet in alarm. In a group by the door stood P.C. Dawson, notebook in hand. *There was no way out.*

Rex Swanley, man-about-suburbia, was also there. He was gripping Brenda's arm. She no longer wore the necklace.

Graham groaned in self-reproach for having incriminated his girlfriend.

He approached the constable. "Let me explain, officer—"

But Brenda had released herself from Rex Swanley's grip and now took Graham aside. "Let me explain," she whispered. "Constable Dawson is here at Cecil Lancaster's invitation. Cecil mistook the constable for an attractive young lady and insisted on bringing him to the party!"

"The necklace?" Graham stammered.

"That's all over and done with. I went to Rex Swanley's house and slipped it in a hallstand drawer, while he was putting his overcoat on."

"But why should Swanley put his overcoat on at one o'clock in the morning?"

Brenda smiled. "An hour ago I was ordered to bring a stranger to the party. Seeing that a call to Hulstone Lodge enabled me to return the necklace, Rex Swanley was clearly the perfect stranger!"

As if attuned to Graham's sudden happiness, the hubbub died down. The Life-and-soul-of-the-party closed the policeman's notebook and offered him a drink. Cecil Lancaster went outside on another quest for pretty girls or lamp-posts. Some bright spark turned out the lights.

Graham embraced Brenda until the lights came on again.

R.S.V.P. to Peggy

Peggy sensed that something was amiss when she came down to breakfast. Grandma forgot to kiss her good morning, and Peggy could not remember that ever happening before. For another thing, Grandma was not smiling as usual, and not even talking.

Peggy wondered whether it had anything to do with the letter which lay beside Grandma's plate. If so, it was a great pity, because the envelope had a lovely coloured stamp; it would look well in the stamp album which Daddy had given her for her sixth birthday.

As Peggy was eating her breakfast in silence, Grandma would pick up the letter, read it through, put it down, sip her coffee, and then pick up the letter again. The fifth time she read it, Peggy noticed, she had it upside down.

At last Grandma spoke. This was after she cleared her throat briskly and hastily dabbed her eyes with her handkerchief. "Excuse me, dear," she said. "I seem to have a cold coming."

Then there was more silence.

Peggy did not like the silence, because she wanted to tell Grandma all about her dream. Daddy had captured ten lions single-handed and sent them straight off, by aeroplane, to the Zoo, so that Peggy could go along and see them.

She did not really expect the dream to come true, of course, because although Daddy was in Africa she knew he was too busy to go anywhere near the jungle.

Even though Daddy had been away for four years, it was easy to dream up a picture of him, for there was a huge photograph in the drawing room. He had a nice kind face, with eyes wide apart that seemed to be smiling at you even more than the face itself.

On the other hand, Peggy had forgotten what her mother had looked like, ever since the picture had been taken down from the wall three years ago, when Mummy had died.

Daddy was something in the Civil Service and had been sent to Africa by the Government. Peggy had never forgiven them for this, and vowed that when she grew up she would never vote for the Government.

Although she liked Grandma very much, Peggy wished she could have gone to Africa with her parents. Bu they had gone to a horrid place that used to be called the White Man's Grave, and it seemed that children were not allowed to live there unless they happened to be born black. It had even accounted for Mummy dying....

Suddenly Grandma spoke again, in that gentle voice she used; not a crackling, old-sounding voice like so many grandmothers. "Whatever are you thinking about child, with that faraway look in your eyes?" She did not wait for an answer, but glanced at the clock and exclaimed: "Goodness gracious! Whatever am *I* thinking about? It's time you were off to school."

During the day Peggy gradually forgot all about the letter. There was plenty of fun at school these days. The hard winter had set in early, and with two weeks still to go before Christmas, snow had settled inches deep. It was as if the earth had suddenly come out in full blossom.

There was all the excitement of snowball fights and toboggan rides. And, with the end of term in sight, even lessons were easy-going, with the strictest teachers behaving like favourite aunts.

So it was not until Peggy returned home in the late afternoon that she remembered about the letter. When Grandma opened the door she was still unsmiling and her eyes were red-rimmed.

Peggy put her arms around Grandma and nestled her pigtailed head against the other's pretty-coloured apron. "What's the matter, Grandma? You've been crying."

"Nonsense, sweetheart," Grandma said with a big smile. "I've been peeling onions."

She changed the subject in the impolite way grown-ups sometimes had. "Now tell me what you've been doing at school today."

Dinner was a more pleasant meal than breakfast had been. Grandma kept up a flow of conversation the whole time... until

Peggy started to tell her about last night's dream. At the mention of Daddy she was suddenly silent.

Peggy was sure now that something was wrong, but she waited until Grandma came to tuck her up in bed before saying anything. Then she asked wistfully: "Why *have* you been crying today?"

"Bless you, child. I told you it was the onions."

"Well, it's a funny thing," Peggy said. "We didn't have onions for dinner. Do tell me, *please*."

Grandma sat on the edge of the bed and said slowly, as though deciding the best words to use, "They were tears of joy, darling. At the good news. Your father's coming home next week!"

Peggy squealed with delight.

"And he's bringing you an extra-special Christmas present."

Peggy clapped her hands. "I know. A walkie talkie doll."

"Oh, no, something far more exciting. He's bringing you a new Mummy. They're going to stay here over Christmas, and then they are taking you to a lovely new house, and will never leave you again. Isn't that wonderful?"

"Are you coming too, Grandma?"

"Well, no. Somebody has to live in this house. In any case, your new Mummy is the one to look after you now."

At this, Peggy's excitement fizzled out like a damp squib. "Who says so?" she asked defiantly.

"The law says so, and the law knows what's best. Besides, I'll often come and visit you."

Grandma went on to describe the wonderful things the four of them would do on those occasions. At length, Peggy fell asleep with a smile....

The days just before Christmas always seemed to drag, but Peggy had never known such long drawn out days as these. Not even the delights of school breaking-up, with snow fights, pantomimes, and parties, could make the hours go more quickly.

"Daddy's coming home." She repeated this to herself every time the clock's hands appeared to stay in the same place.

Daddy's coming home. In seven days' time.

In six days, twelve hours' time.

In five days' time.

Often she would pinch herself to make sure it was not one of those silly dreams which had a habit of never coming true.

But it was real enough. She knew that from the funny feeling she had every time she thought about it—like a bunch of butterflies whisking inside her.

But what about this new Mummy? Would she really like her, as Grandma had told her hundreds of times she would? And anyhow, why wouldn't Grandma still look after her? If the law said she couldn't, the law jolly well ought to mind its own business.

Four days.

Two days.

Tomorrow!

Tomorrow never comes, people said. But this tomorrow better had!

And come it did, at long last. And with it came a handsome middle-aged man, a beautiful lady who looked ten years younger than Daddy, and a pile of suitcases. Most of them seemed to contain the lady's dresses.

Peggy opened the door to them, and was immediately swallowed up into her father's arms. "My word, you've grown," he said huskily. "Look, Daphne, this is your new daughter."

The new Mummy smiled as she kissed Peggy. But the kiss was not as firm as Daddy's. And the smile did not make her feel warm inside, as Daddy's did, even though it showed up a set of pearly-white teeth, none in the least uneven.

Peggy was not sure whether she liked this new Mummy. Of course she was beautiful. But her short dark hair was pushed back from her face and ears, so that it was not even as wavy as Grandma's.

"Hello, Mummy," Peggy said shyly.

"Hello, Peggy. I'm sure we're going to be friends." The beautiful lady spoke like a wireless announcer. "But I want you to call me *Mother*. I think *Mummy* is childish."

Peggy swallowed hard. "All right... M-Mother."

Now that the great day of Daddy's return had come and gone, the next event to look forward to was Christmas Day in a week's time.

Peggy had to make a start on her annual composition—a letter to Santa Claus. This pleasant task (as far as the actual writing was concerned) was all her own work; but Grandma usually helped her with a hint or two. Grandma was very clever at this because Santa Claus always seemed to bring the things that she suggested. This year she had suggested a walkie talkie doll.

Peggy did not usually think ahead for more than a week or two. But as she was writing this year's letter a thought occurred: What about next year? Grandma would not be living with them then. Try as she might, Peggy could not imagine the new Mummy joining in a letter to Santa Claus.

Peggy felt sad at the thought. As indeed she felt sad at many such thoughts nowadays.

Never mind, though. Only four days to Christmas.

Three days.... Two days.

It was Christmas Eve, and the snow was falling in huge flakes on the bedroom window.

Peggy was watching the flakes through half-closed eyes, when Daddy and the new Mummy came in together to say goodnight.

"Look, darling, she's asleep," Daddy said. "I expect the excitement was too much for her."

Peggy closed her eyes firmly, playing a game of make-believe.

"She looks so innocent, Daphne, it seems a pity to send her away to a boarding school," Daddy was saying. "At least, until she's a good deal older."

Daphne replied sharply. "We've had all this out before, Bernard. Remember, I have my career to think of."

"But there's no need for you to go into business, Daphne. This new post of mine will provide for us amply. If you must have added interests you can join societies, committees, take up welfare work. You're so good at that sort of thing."

"Then that wouldn't leave me sufficient time to look after Peggy at home."

"You know the answer to that, darling. We can live in this house—there's no need to move. Mother can help you look after Peggy. You must admit she's made a pretty good job of it so far, and it's a pity to part them."

Daphne spoke quite crossly. "No, Bernard. I will not have the child growing up with Victorian ideas."

"Nonsense!" was the sharp reply. Then—"We'd better go, Peggy's stirring."

The closing of the door muffled Peggy's sobs. What a Christmas Eve this was, she thought bitterly. All the happiness wiped out in one sweep by a new Mummy who did not understand her. She could not get to sleep now, but it was not the excitement which kept her awake.

She lay for hours, just thinking, and bravely trying to stifle the sobs which came into her throat.

At length, she felt she would be happier in the nursery, where she could dwell for a while in the world of her daydreams. So she slipped out of bed, put on her bedroom slippers, and also her outdoor coat—for the night was cold—and crept along to the nursery. There she sat in her favourite chair, to think....

She had not been sitting there long before she heard a great rush and hustle about the house. Voices were raised excitedly. Daddy was saying: "You phone the police, Daphne, while I find a torch. And we'll need some blankets. No, Mother, you are not to come out. You can have some hot water ready for a bath and hot coffee when we return. Pray God she's not gone far."

What a commotion, Peggy thought. Still, grown-ups always made noises at night. They lived in a world of their own after the children were abed. Well, tonight *she* was staying up late, and living in a world of *her* own.

She went over to her desk....

An hour later, Peggy awoke to find herself in Daddy's arms. He was wearing his outdoor clothes, and his face was as white as the snow on his overcoat.

Mummy was with him, and looking just as worried. Peggy had never seen her looking so human.

Daddy said: "Why didn't we think of looking in here first!"

As he leaned over her, he saw the letter she had been writing at the desk. It was pencilled in a tremulous scrawl, and there were untidy streaks where the tears had merged with indelible lead. Strangely moved, he read:

"Dear Santa Claus—Please don't think I'm a turncoat, but I've changed my mind about the walkie talkie doll. Also the pencil box and paints I asked for. Don't bring me anything at all.

"All I want is you to make my new Mummy understand me, and let me not have to call her Mother. Also let Mummy take up well fair work, so that we can all live here. Daddy, Mummy, Grandma, and Me."

Bernard passed the note to Daphne. "R.S.V.P.," he whispered.

In a moment of rare insight, Daphne saw just how much Bernard meant to her. She saw how much Peggy's "disappearance" and now the letter, meant to Bernard. And because of those values, she knew just how much Peggy meant to them all.

Daphne said to Peggy, gently, "We've just been out to meet Santa Claus. He knows about the letter, and he says the answer is 'Yes.' "

Peggy fell asleep, with a smile.

Return Journey

The 1912-vintage engine chugged a protest, as it hauled up the steep gradient more carriages than was good for it.

From his corner seat, Roderick Marsh chuckled in appreciation. "It's a long time since I travelled this line," he said. "But I can guess why they put these ancient engines in service."

"Well, *I* can't," Brenda snapped. She was anxious to reach Brandonville-on-Sea before evening—a target which British Railways did not seem to share.

Roderick smiled. "It's simple really. The scenery is so intoxicating round these parts that they want travellers to drink it in, in sips, not to quaff it."

Roderick, at 50, was still the lover of beauty he had been at 30, when he last came to Brandonville. That was before they were married.

In fact, as he reminded Brenda now, it was in a secluded cave in Brandonville that he had proposed.

At this idyllic reminder, Brenda's irritation momentarily passed. "That was the most enjoyable evening of my life," she murmured. Then—with another swift change of mood—"But I do wish this wretched train would get us there again. As you know, I went to Brandonville last year, and it's more wonderful than ever."

"Yes of course, darling," said the lover of beauty.

Brenda came within the beauty category too. Her features were still in the same classic mould of 20 years ago, when he had proposed undying love in the cave under Deadman's Rock. And her sylphlike figure belied her 45 years.

But Roderick also enjoyed the beauties of nature, and despite the pressing attentions of his fair companion, he turned again to look out of the window.

To one side were luxuriant woods, where pines, poplar and silver birch stood proudly on a carpet of moss and fern. Through the wood, like a sliver of mercury, a stream ran parallel to the railway lines;

and a shoal of fish, too small to interest the angler, were visible through the crystal-clear water, as, untroubled, they hunted for food.

Beyond the wood, the ground rose sharply, and the Five Sisters stood as sentinels of nature's paradise. The Five Sisters were a series of downs, spaced an equal distance apart and of a symmetry to excite the mathematician as well as the artist. They were burial mounds of 2,000 years ago, but—emerald after the spring rains—there was nothing funereal about them now.

Roderick sipped the scenery, which to an office-based stockbroker was nectar of the gods. The view presented a kaleidoscope of colour as well as of contour, and the faithful chugging engine, as it followed the frequent curve of railway lines, was the hand which shook the kaleidoscope. Woodland changed to farmland, and the farmers in these parts—paying homage to the panorama—had arranged their several plots in suitably scenic fashion, the dividing lines of hedgerow and rustic fencing forming a pleasing jigsaw.

The engine chugged on. Here a 17th century village flecked the railway line, there a cluster of thatched cottages.

Roderick was hardly aware of Brenda's presence as—without so much as a glance out of the window—she sidled closer. He was not even aware of the hand that took his in a caressing clasp, or of the kiss that alighted like a butterfly on the side of his face which was not turned to the window.

Subconsciously, however, romance was stirred, because his thoughts suddenly switched five miles distant to the end of the journey, and 20 years back in time. To the cave in Deadman's Rock where he had asked Brenda to marry him.

He thought of Brandonville's magnificent bay—a shallow dish of handsome design, containing lagoon-blue waters whose like could not be seen this side of the South Seas. Of the small boats which sailed those waters, and the surf-riding craft when the sea was less kind and bubbled up into foam-crested waves.

He thought, too, of the grandeur of rugged rock, where lovers walked for miles with only the seagulls as companions. And of the caves within those rocks where not even the seagull would venture.

Of the quaint winding streets, with their small general stores— each one a curiosity shop—and the quiet so-called main road with its beautiful church which could boast a lineage back to Norman times.

Brenda also thought of Brandonville-on-Sea. But her reflections were concentrated on an impatience to get there.

At last the gallant engine reached its goal, and with something of a sigh nosed against the buffers of Brandonville station.

Roderick knew it as a small station, but now it was almost a junction. The bustle of porters, the screech of taxis, and the stream of humanity damped his nostalgic reflections like a blanket.

Outside the barrier, the winding streets had been straightened and widened; the old curiosity shops were super markets, and a palais de dance nestled against the Norman church.

Along the promenade it was no better. Bazaars and amusement arcades, garish in their neon and chrome, obscured the rocks and the marine gardens. Motor boats churned the blue waters, and golden sands had been transformed to an oil-burdened grey.

Roderick was furious. "What d'you think of this, this sacrilege?" he spluttered.

"It's wonderful," Brenda replied. "Let's go to the hotel and change, try our luck on the pin tables, and then go on to the palais de dance."

Roderick looked hard at her, and with an air of finality, said, "You've changed with Brandonville. I'm glad you refused me when I proposed 20 years ago. I'm going back to my wife, and I suggest you go back to your husband."

Return to Sender

The message came whilst Alaric Jayson was making his third business call that day. His client's secretary interrupted the discussion to report: "Your office on the phone, Mr. Jayson—been trying to get you all day—they want you to return right away."

Jayson shrugged his thin shoulders as if to emphasise his self-importance, and quickly donned his long-service bowler hat. The smile which creased his weak features was one of apology for premature departure, but it was a barely-concealed grin of triumph, and he hurried away lest his client should observe the malevolent gleam in his weak blue eyes.

Outside in the street, Jayson boarded a bus. A taxi would have been more fitting perhaps, in view of the urgency, but he needed the extra time to compose his nerves… and to bolster-up his nerve.

For when he arrived at the office, they would tell him that old Parsloe, the chief clerk, was dead. And he, Jayson, must feign a surprise which in the peculiar circumstances he could not possibly feel.

Whittingham, the young managing director, would then proceed to offer him the chief clerk vacancy. Jayson was sure of that. Long years as understudy to old Parsloe meant automatic promotion now that the chief clerk was dead.

As the bus crawled comfortably along, Jayson's thoughts raced ahead, with bubbling anticipation, to his homecoming that evening. If Whittingham were to promote him that afternoon, he need fear Clarissa's tongue no longer.

His wife would begin her nightly nagging session as usual: "You've stagnated far too long in that blind-alley job, Alaric."—"I can't think why I married a worm who hasn't the guts to change his job at forty."—"How d'you expect me to keep up with the Joneses and the Robinsons on a Jaysons' salary?" And so on. And on.

Blind-alley job, eh? Yes, it was true. But now that the brick wall at the end of the alley—in the shape of old Parsloe—had been removed, the way ahead was clear. He would be able to keep up with the Joneses and the Robinsons and, what was more important, with Clarissa.

Jayson had first decided to murder Mr. Parsloe over a month ago, when on approaching retirement age the chief clerk (enjoying disgustingly good health) had elected to stay on another five years. The main problem had been the method of killing. Poisons were hard to come by; accidents difficult to arrange. Violence was out of the question; Jayson's shrivelled-up little soul shrank at the thought of laying hands on the bigger man, and he couldn't trust even a pistol distance between them.

Eventually, he had capitalised on his service with the Bomb Disposal Squad. During the war, he had picked up sufficient technical detail to produce his own home-made bomb. So! He would blow Parsloe up—from a safe distance!

Over the past weeks he had secured the materials piece by piece, so that they couldn't be traced back to him. And yesterday, he had put the plan into operation.

The bomb was in the form of a business package addressed to the firm, marked for the personal attention of Mr. Parsloe. Jayson had registered the parcel, doubly to ensure that the chief clerk alone should open it. It had been an idiosyncrasy of old Parsloe's that no menial hand should touch a registered package.

Wearing a simple but effective disguise, Jayson had dispatched the parcel from a main post office, where in any case he was unlikely to be identified later from amongst a crowd.

The parcel-bomb should have arrived that morning, which was why Jayson had arranged interviews out of the office. (There was no point in being about when the bomb went off!) And now had come this urgent summons back the office, and in about five minutes' time he was going to reap the reward of his endeavours.

Jayson alighted from the bus, to walk the remaining 100 yards to his office in a side street, bracing himself up to receive *the news*. Of a sudden, an icicle of fear played a tattoo on his jellied spine and he faltered in his stride. Supposing the shrewd Whittingham's urgent summons was not one of promotion but one of accusation?

It was only after a frantic mental 're-capping' of the situation, and just as he was about to enter the building, what Jayson remembered the post office receipt for the registered parcel. Of course! He had retained it instead of destroying it. One of those automatic actions which the most careful of planning is apt to overlook; a thread which could have woven a rope about his neck! Hastily, he took the fateful slip of paper from his wallet and tore it into a myriad shreds.

In a sweat of relief intermingled with apprehension, he entered the managing director's office. "Good afternoon, sir, I've been hurrying," he said breathlessly, to explain away his perspiration. "I understand you want me urgently."

"Ah yes, old chap," Whittingham greeted him pleasantly. "I need your help. Draw up a chair, will you?"

False alarm. Jayson congratulated himself.

"You see," the managing director explained, "Mr. Parsloe is away today—"

"Not dead, I hope," said Jayson involuntarily.

"Good heavens, whatever makes you say that? It's a chill—"

Despite his relief, a string of curses surged through Jayson's taut mind; wisely unspoken ones. For now the murder would have to be postponed, and with it his domestic triumph over Clarissa.

"—And so," Whittingham went on, "I'm tackling Parsloe's paper work; but I must confess some of the routine is beyond me, so I've called you back to assist. Now what do you think of this Bartlett & Swanson tender?"

Together behind the great desk, the two men worked at the absent Parsloe's papers. But the advice Jayson was proffering seemed hardly worthy of a potential chief clerk. He couldn't concentrate, for an uneasy presentiment was battering at his subconscious. What danger still lay ahead? What was it he had to guard against? Ah, of course, *the parcel.* Somehow he must intercept it, and hide it away pending Parsloe's return to the office.

The incisive tones of Mr. Whittingham cut into Jayson's troubled thoughts. "We don't seem to be making much headway, Mr. Jayson. And the time's getting on. Perhaps we'd better dictate replies to those letters we've dealt with." The managing director pressed the buzzer on his desk to summon his secretary.

Miss Slater entered the room, carrying a shorthand notebook in one hand; in the other hand—a parcel. Jayson quailed in his chair as he recognised the contours of the sinister boxed-shaped package. So much for his hopes of interception.

"I brought in this parcel, Mr. Whittingham," said the girl. "It's marked for Mr. Parsloe's attention, but seeing Mr. Jayson in here, I thought he might be able to deal with it. Although," she added speculatively, "it's probably only samples."

"That's right," Jayson echoed gratefully. "It's probably only samples. I'll—I'll open it later."

At this sign of dithering, Mr. Whittingham lost something of his geniality. "I pay you to deduce facts, Mr. Jayson," he snapped. "Not to estimate probabilities. Surely the thing to do is to open the package and to be sure of its contents.

"Now, Miss Slater, we'll start the first letter while Mr. Jayson is ascertaining his facts. 'Dear Sirs, In response to—' " The managing director stopped short in mid-sentence. "Where the devil are you off to, Jayson? I'll want you to help me with the correspondence."

"I'm going to my own office to fetch a knife," replied the deputy-chief clerk, who had risen from his chair, the parcel clutched under his arm.

"My own pen-knife is at your elbow," Whittingham said, acidly. "Is not that sharp enough?"

"Er yes, sir. I mean, no sir, I—I can't seem to cut the string."

"Here, man, let me do it! There seems to be something of a mystery about that parcel."

The managing director leaned across the desk and began to open the parcel. In the split seconds that elapsed whilst the knife was poised, Jayson's mental responses worked overtime. It would be equally dangerous whichever of the two men opened the package: in such proximity they would both be killed. He could, of course, run out of the office; but then Miss Slater, who was sitting a safe distance away, would live to bear testimony against him.

Only one course would save his miserable skin: confession to the attempted murder of old Parsloe, with the inevitable ten-years-plus term of imprisonment.

The managing director had cut the string and was about to unravel the brown paper, when, like a man demented, Jayson grabbed his arm. "STOP!" he screamed. "Don't open that parcel."

"And why not, Jayson?"

Sentence by pitiful sentence, Jayson blurted out the whole story, whilst the efficient Miss Slater made rapid shorthand notes. When he had concluded his confession, Jayson grovelled: "You'll put in a good word for me, won't you sir? I can't bear long years in prison."

"Don't worry," the managing director replied. "You won't be in prison very long and the charge won't be attempted murder. I'll see to that."

"You mean you'll keep it dark, sir?"

"I mean," Whittingham replied grimly, "the charge will be *murder*. This parcel on the desk is one I faked-up to trap you. The real parcel-bomb killed poor Parsloe this morning."

"B-but—you said—" Jason was quite incoherent. "P-Parsloe—a chill."

"The chill of death, Jayson. Which I think you will find is infectious."

Saddle-Bagged

His name wasn't Ernest, but it should have been. A more earnest individual had never graced the offices of Messrs. Lock, Stock and Barrel, chartered accountants.

A model citizen was Wilfred. Until identity cards were abolished, he had carried his as religiously as a City man his umbrella. From a picnic he would walk home with his pockets stuffed with paper bags, rather than leave the faintest suspicion of litter. Of course, he always Posted Early for Christmas.

Wilfred was a shade unpopular with his colleagues, who found his high-minded principles somewhat overpowering. As witness the morning he was late for business and signed the attendance book "9:08 a.m." The rest of the staff—who normally arrived at ten past nine, but always signed in "9:00 a.m."—were thus forced to announce their own late arrival.

He was also unpopular with Cupid, who hadn't so much as thrown a dart in his general direction. Wilfred regarded the modern miss as frivolous; something to be avoided like the plague.

Until Cynthia joined the firm.

She breezed into the drab office one day like a shaft of sunlight infiltrating a cellar grating.

"Morning," she greeted Wilfrid snappily. "The boss says I'm to sit opposite you."

At the shock, Wilfred's pince-nez slipped off his nose. Although hitherto he had been unmoved by beauty, this girl had a personality which pierced his misogynistic armour.

"G-good morning, madam," he replied. For the rest of the morning his expression was a judicious blend of goggle-eyed courteousness.

And so, indeed, it was for the rest of the month, because Wilfred was too shy to speak his piece. At 30, he had never even kissed a girl, and in his rigid observance of the conventions he was a throwback to the Victorian era.

At length, he blurted out: "I wonder, Miss Goldsworthy, would you venture to accompany me to the opera one evening?"

"Sure," replied Cynthia, who hated the opera but loved Wilfred. "How about tonight?"

A month later he was bringing her home to tea.

Six months later he was spending the evenings in her home. Gingerly holding hands on the settee, he fought back reckless words of devotion. The time was not yet ripe by his conventional calendar.

When the summer came, the arena of their courtship was extended. Cynthia persuaded Wilfred to take up cycling, and lent him her brother's machine for a trial run.

One glorious Sunday in June found them setting off down the country lanes—the girl riding ahead, Wilfred wobbling behind as though the roadway were a giant cake-walk.

After a picnic spread in a romantic spot, Wilfred read aloud a sonnet of his own composition, to which Cynthia listened with admirable patience. The elements expressed their viewpoint in far more forcible terms. It started to rain.

"There's a barn in the next field!" Cynthia exclaimed. She scampered for shelter, expertly wheeling both bikes as she ran. Wilfred remained to pick up the litter.

While they were in the barn the storm broke, and it was dusk before they could venture out again. Fortunately, Wilfred had a good supply of sonnets....

When at last they made to set off homewards, Cynthia remarked casually: "I don't suppose it will matter about not having any lights. It's a quiet road."

Wilfred was horrified. "Great Scot, we can't ride without lights. It's against the law!"

"Then we'll have to put up for the night," Cynthia said. "I know this locality well. That's Farmer Dagley's house over there."

Wilfred hesitated for a long moment, as an ultra-sensitive convention wrestled with an ultra-civic pride. Citizenship won by the shortest of heads. "Then it will have to be Farmer Dagley's house," he declared.

And Farmer Dagley's house it was.

The next morning they set off home quite early, because Wilfred was anxious not to be late for the office. In the farmyard they saw a milkmaid, who stared at them pointedly and hurried away.

Cynthia said: "That's Farmer Dagley's girl—the county's biggest gossip. She's bound to put a false construction on a perfectly innocent occurrence."

As they wheeled their bikes to the roadway, Wilfred said musingly, "There's only one course now. Having compromised you in the eyes of that suspicious scandalmonger, I must advance my plans and ask you to marry me."

"What a sweet proposal," Cynthia answered. She put one arm round Wilfred's neck and kissed him. With the other arm she tucked the bicycle lamps more securely in her saddlebag.

Second Time Lucky

Tempered by a friendly breeze, the June sunshine smiled down on the busy high street. Towards the middle of the street stood the imposing parish church; and the waves of humanity converging at this point fanned out two deep around the railings. All the world loves a wedding, but no section more so than a Saturday afternoon shopping crowd.

The shiny black Rolls Royce, temporarily hired out on Cupid's service, threaded its way through the knot of traffic. "What a beautiful bride," the crowd chorused. A bridal gown, of course, lends beauty to any wearer, but in the case of Linda Scott the loan was an unsought one. Her dark beauty would have adorned the humblest costume.

Linda was very happy; she was going to marry the most wonderful man in the world. She was convinced that Robert Grayley came into this category, although she had known him for only six months. After all, she told herself, when you are 28 you reckon to know your own mind (and heart) even if you have been so busy building up a career that you haven't bothered unduly with the opposite sex.

Linda relaxed in the car, hardly aware of the remarks of Uncle Roderick, who sat beside her. It was a pity her parents couldn't be at the wedding, she mused, but naturally they couldn't very well make the trip from India (where her father had a government post) at a moment's notice. Never mind, she would send them a copy of the photographs and a piece of the cake; they would be with her in spirit, and it was still the happiest day of her life.

Then, of a sudden, as the Rolls Royce bowled up the church drive, a chill of premonition butterflied within her—to erase in an instant her joy of living. *Why weren't the bells ringing?* And why was Charles standing there on the church steps, when he should have been at the altar lending best-man support to his brother?

From the crowd of sightseers around the railings came a murmur of surprise as Charles stepped down to meet the car and to direct the driver round to the secluded side entrance. When the car finally pulled up to a halt, Charles opened the doors and with a significant nod, beckoned Uncle Roderick outside. Then he himself got into the car beside Linda.

"Hello," she laughed uncertainly. "Have you forgotten the ring?"

Charles shook his head and regarded her gravely for a moment, wondering how to put into words the message that had no part of a best man's normal duties—one which figured in no etiquette book on the subject. Finally he chose the direct approach: "You won't need the ring, Linda. I'm afraid the wedding's off."

"Oh!" Linda gasped. "Has anything happened to Bob?"

Charles took her hand in his, with an awkward sort of tenderness. "Bob's fine, thanks. It's just that he felt at the very last moment that what he had mistaken for love... just wasn't. It's fairer to you both, he says, not to go through with it."

"I see." What a mundane expression that was! But Linda *did* see—very clearly. And to see was to understand. "Bob couldn't have noted otherwise," she reassured Charles.

"I tried to hold up the car before it reached your house," Charles went on, "but I was too late. So I slipped back to the church to meet you here. And now that you are here, Linda, the family insist you come home to stay with us... for as long as you like.

"Don't worry," he added, as Linda shook her dark curls. "Bob's gone away for a while."

"It's not that, Charles. I'd rather face this thing on my own. Please tell the driver to take me to back to my flat. Thank your family all the same, and thank *you*."

Linda was oblivious of the curious stares of the sightseers as the car turned tail. Already she had decided how to cope with the situation; she would try as best she could to carry on as though Bob had never entered her life. The less she dwelt on the incident, the less the heartache and the sooner the healing.

Home again, she went at once to her bedroom and changed into some "sensible" clothes. A pair of slacks and an old woolly jumper were more sensible, certainly, for the task on hand—which was to give the flat its weekly spring-clean. For the next hour or so, Linda busied herself about the house, the whirr of the vacuum cleaner co-operating nicely to stifle the whirr of her thoughts. Relentlessly, she stumped about the place, polishing here, scrubbing there, the very vigour of her graceful arms combatting the blows of fate.

Sunday dawned so clearly and brightly that Linda took the train to the nearest coast town—her favourite haunt of pre-courtship days. If during the day she was reminded of the contrast between this resort and the French Riviera—where she should now have been honeymooning—well, she shook off those thoughts with a toss of her head and a jutting out of shapely chin.

On Monday morning came the vital test. Over the weekend Linda had decided, after a long fight with her irresolution, to return to her old job. So, after the usual hasty breakfast, she helter-skeltered down to the tube station; a short sharp walk at the other end, and she was entering once again the huge grey block of buildings across which was blazoned in gilt letters: CRAMER FOR COSMETICS..

But for all the self-assurance which habit afforded, Linda entered the office hesitantly, then scurried past the receptionist's desk before that young lady could bombard her with awkward questions. It was with all the trepidation of a junior seeking rise that Linda tapped on the door marked GERALD KIRKWALL – CHIEF BUYER. When she had last entered that office, as Mr. Kirkwall's secretary, Linda had flounced into the room; now she floundered.

But that Gerald Kirkwall was the awe-inspiring type. He was indeed the most human of the firm's executives, and with it, the most popular and most efficient. And incidentally, at 35, the youngest.

"*Hello*, there, Linda," was his surprised greeting. (He had never used the Christian name before.) "Er… Miss Scott, I should say. No, wrong again, I should say Mrs. Robert Grayley."

Linda took a chair facing the big desk. How strange to be sitting here minus her notebook and plus her hat and coat! "You were right first time, Mr. Kirkwall. I'm still plain Linda Scott."

"'Plain' is not the adjective I should choose, but no matter; tell me, what has happened?"

"Well, nothing much," Linda white-lied. My fiancé was taken ill—nothing serious—but the wedding's off for at least six months. And—"

"Hard luck," said Gerald. "And?"

"And I wondered if I could have my old job back. That is to say," Linda concluded in a rush of words that she herself would have found difficult to take down in shorthand. "If it's not inconvenient, and if it's not too irregular."

"We-e-ell." Despite his calm bearing, Gerald couldn't hold back an expression of surprise, and—was it?—annoyance. "That's a shade awkward, Miss Scott. The fact is—"

"You have a replacement already, Mr. Kirkwall?"

"Replacement? Ah, yes that's it! I have a replacement, Miss Scott."

"Then I won't keep you," said Linda, rising quickly to hide her disappointment; and before Gerald could say another word she turned and left the office.

Her next port of call was the estate agent's office. In the weekend whirl of abnormal normality, she had up to this moment completely forgotten that she had given notice to quit her flat. She must resolve the matter at once.

The estate agent was the sole executive in *his* firm, but had there been others he would undoubtedly have been the least human and the most unpopular He didn't even offer Linda a chair. "Renew the lease, Miss Scott?" he said in "the customer's-always-wrong" tones. "That, I'm afraid, would be tantamount to asking for the Koh-i-noor Diamond. I've already let the flat at the end of the month, and there are a hundred people lined up for it after that. Of course, if you wish to be added to the list and would care to pay a fee of five guineas—"

But Linda had gone.

Dorothy Danson's Employment Bureau, where Linda called next, was an agency much favoured by her previous employers. There, she asked if they had "something in the Cosmetics line."

"I have just one vacancy, madam," said the receptionist— "Cramer Cosmetics Limited, contact Gerald Kirkwall, Chief Buyer."

Linda smiled. "I happen to know the position is now filled."

"Oh, no, you're mistaken, madam. I was speaking to Mr. Kirkwall only a minute or two ago. He still wants a replacement for a secretary who left to get married."

Linda forced another smile, although a tear would have been a truer reflection of her feelings. "Thank you all the same, I shouldn't care to work at Cramer's."

Over a cup of tea in a nearby restaurant, Linda worked out her problem a stage further. It seemed that her plan to combat fate in a "business-as-usual" basis was being countered by fate itself. For one brief moment she plumbed the depths of utter despair—deserted by her lover, unwanted by her employer, ignored by her landlord. What was there to live for?

Linda Scott being a girl of spirit, the answer came in flash. Everything! If the way ahead was blocked, then she must take the detour that circumstances demanded. And perhaps Dorothy Danson's Employment Bureau might yet serve as the signpost.

She called again on the agency. "Have you anything out of town?" she asked. "I don't mind how far off it is."

The receptionist drew out a card from her file index. "How about this one, madam? A post with a Cosmetics Company in Dalverton— and there's a flat to go with the job!"

"Made to measure," Linda murmured. She left the agency in a happier frame of mind; and with the aid of an introduction card to the firm in question, a rail ticket to Dalverton and a batch of glowing references, she secured the post.

The next six months slipped by so quickly that Linda hardly had time to bemoan her fate. During that period, thanks to a resolute heart-free application to business, she rose to the position of Sales Manager; thus creating a precedent in the annals of the firm.

Dalverton was a pleasant place, as provincial towns go, with some delightful excursion spots; and in the course of time, Linda was treading these romantic places in romantic company. With one accord the masculine escorts spoke of love and marriage, which showed their good sense and sound logic, but Linda's response was a guarded refusal to discuss such alien terms. Whenever she trod the path of romance, she was followed by the shadow of the wedding that never came off. Pleasant company she was indeed, but as platonic as a maiden aunt.

Dining alone at her favourite restaurant one evening—a pleasant little place, both exclusive and secluded—she was startled to hear her name spoken. "May I join your table, please, Linda?"

She turned sharply. "BOB! What are you doing here?" What *was* Bob doing here? Why did he have to come to open up again the wound which Time had all but healed? "What are you doing here?" she repeated almost angrily.

"Finding you, my dearest, after months of search. You really should have left a forwarding address."

Linda's frown quickly smoothed out to a smile. "And now that you've found me?"

"I want to propose all over again. Linda, darling, will you marry me?"

Her heart leaped; bluebirds were singing; everything in the garden was lovely. Her lips formed the one word of magic affirmative, but no sound came. The sun—as suddenly as it had appeared in the garden of her life—had dipped again behind a cloud. Instinctively, she studied Bob as though seeing him for the first time. A likeable fellow, with frank honest features, but with a boyish immaturity still outlined on his handsome face, an immaturity which her past infatuation had overlooked.

In reflective silence, Linda stirred the coffee cup before her. She saw Robert Grayley as a creature of impulse. Impulse it was that had first led him to propose after a brief acquaintance; that had later prompted him to cancel the wedding; and that now had urged him to propose for the second time.

Bob regarded her with a perplexed frown. "I think you've stirred that coffee long enough. Why not add a little sweetness to my life?" Misinterpreting her silence, he added: "Don't worry, dear, I won't let you down again."

"There never has been any 'let-down,' Bob. You have always acted for the best. It so happens that your wedding day decision was the right one for both of us, but I was too blind to see it then."

Bob sighed. "A wasted trip to Dalverton—"

"Not wasted," Linda replied gently. "I'm grateful for your making the trip and for opening my eyes to the truth of my heart...."

Linda coaxed sleep in vain that night. The shadow of the wedding was now taking definition. Bob was eliminated as a diagnosis for her heartache, and that left—only Gerald Kirkwall, the man with whom for years she had worked, laughed, shared problems, a man with a youthful outlook but a mature mind. In short—the man she loved. What mattered if he acted hastily over the question of re-engaging her as his secretary? What mattered anything, other than that she loved him?

And could it be that her love was returned? There came suddenly memory flashes of conversations, odd hints here and there which at the time had gone right over her head and certainly over her heart. Could it be...?

Linda had some compensation for her sleeplessness, in the shape of one of those brilliant inspirations which come only in the still watches of the night. And so on the following morning, acting on that inspiration, she summoned to her office her assistant sales manager. "Mr. Welles, I want you to draft a circular letter advertising our new lipstick, to go out under my signature."

"Very good, Miss Scott. To the usual list of addresses?"

"We might expand the field this time, Mr. Welles. Include, er... Handbag Accessories Limited and people like that, and... oh... Cramer Cosmetics, for the attention of their Chief Buyer—a Mr. Kirkwall, I believe...."

A week later, a client was summoned into Linda's office. *"Hello,*
there, Gerald," she exclaimed, adding mischievously, "er... I should
say, Mr. *Kirkwall.*"

The visitor shook her hand warmly and replied, "Right first time,
because it is as 'Gerald' that I'm about to ask you out to lunch.
Although as your potential client, you should be asking me!"

They went along to the secluded restaurant round the corner and
over the meal spoke freely and naturally about old times, until by the
coffee stage the conversation had worked its way to present day
events. "So you got my circular letter?" Linda asked, now a little
nervously.

"Oh, yes. And incidentally I have a letter for you, Linda." Gerald
handed over an envelope whose face was scarred by innumerable
crossings-out. It was addressed to Mrs. Robert Grayley, c/o the hotel
in France where she had planned to spend her honeymoon. The hotel
manager had re-addressed the letter to Bob's home.

Bob, in turn, had forwarded it to Linda's old flat. From there, it
had been marked *Gone Away* and eventually had been dealt with by
the Post Office: *Return to Sender.*

"And I, being the sender," Gerald said, "am taking the
opportunity of delivering it to you in person."

Dear Mrs. Grayley, (read the letter) *Just a few lines to
congratulate you on your wedding, and to say that I think your
husband is the most fortunate man in the world. I envy him!*

"You can see why I wasn't anxious to have you working with me
again," Gerald said.

"Knowing that the letter, revealing my feelings as it did, was on
its way to you, it would have been altogether too embarrassing, and
not in the least good for business."

Linda cleared her throat hastily. "About my firm's circular letter,"
she said. "Have you come up with any orders?"

"Just one order," whispered Gerald. "I want you to marry me; and
I want to take an early delivery."

Linda leaned across the table and kissed Gerald gently. "That was the official acknowledgement, darling," she murmured. "And delivery can be very prompt. You see… I happen to have a wedding dress already made."

+

Stags at Bay

The stag party was not going with a swing. Joe Rickard could hardly be faulted on his account; he had installed his four guests in deep armchairs around a bright fire in the luxurious Mayfair flat. A tasty cold collation was within arms' easy reach; and wine and cigars were available *ad lib.*

For all that, the guests (each a social success in his own sphere) could not find the common denominator for camaraderie. Silently they viewed each other with a mutually shifty eye, for beneath the veneer of their social standing ran the streak of a guilty secret. Did they but know it, here *was* a common denominator for the asking: they were all being blackmailed by the same man.

Rickard, whose face, by contrast, bore a pleasant but cynical grin, handed round the ham sandwiches. "Another sandwich for you, Evans?"

"No, damn you," muttered the young businessman. "Your food sticks in my throat."

"Evans, my dear fellow," Rickard remonstrated, "if your clients hear you talk like that you'll soon be out of business."

"I will be in any case"—Evans was quite distraught—"the way I'm being bled."

"What about you, colonel?"

"Yes, I'll have a sandwich," the old soldier rasped, "but only because it suits me. I'm hungry."

Webbly, the shrewd little solicitor, shook his head. "No, thank you, Mr.—Er—Mr.—?"

"Call me Mr. X," spluttered Webbly; incensed by his host's cynical grin, and emboldened by the evidence of his fellow-guests' plight, he continued: "When you find yourself in the dock, you will hear *us* referred to as Mr. X. You will be cited as the dastardly blackmailer."

Rickard waved the suggestion aside, his long, slender fingers caressing the air. "You will never prosecute, Mr. Weebly. There's too great a risk to disclosure of your little embezzlement act—"

"Have a sandwich, Mr. Jarlin."

"Cut the cackle," the portly member of the gathering replied. He glanced fussily at his watch. "I'm due to address an election meeting shortly. Tell us why you have brought us here."

"Since you ask, I will tell you." Rickard smiled. "Month by month you have all been paying out to a blackmailer you have only seen behind a mask—to a man whose name you do not know. So I thought I would ask you all here tonight and we can have a jolly get-together."

"You swine," said the colonel. "What's your game?" Haven't you bled us enough?"

"Hush, colonel. Your language is not so tender as that displayed in your indiscreet love letters.

"Well, gentlemen," Rickard continued, "a party is not complete without presents, and I have one for you all."

He went over to a magnificent bookcase standing over on the far side of the room, and took out a briefcase. From this he extracted a number of small bundles of documents. "Here, colonel, is the batch of love letters under discussion. Don't do it again, there's a good soldier.

"Here, Mr. Jarlin M.P., are some marriage certificates showing your partiality for a girl in every constituency. Kindly stick to one partner in future.

"Mr. Webbly—your record of embezzlement. Keep a stricter account in future.

"And for you, Mr. Evans, some documents which illustrate some interesting but illegal share-pushing deals. For now on, you'd better mind your own business."

Whilst they were all pocketing their precious records with incredulous and grateful amazement, young Evans burst out, "It's a trap. I know it is. He's had photostat copies made of all these papers."

Evans sprang to his feet and leapt across the carpet, his hand to Rickard's throat.

"Stop him!" the solicitor yelled. "If he murders the cad, we'll all be charged as accessories before the fact."

The colonel, ever the man of action, rushed to pull Evans off; but the aid was unsought; with tigerish strength, Rickard had flung the assailant aside.

"Now don't be hasty, gentlemen," he said. (His smile was still in place.) "I was about to add that... I am one of you, a blackmailing victim. Something to do with a spot of safe-breaking I perpetrated in a misspent youth. The only difference is: you've all paid through the nose for years. I don't intend to start.

"Our blackmailer friend lives near here; I invited him here tonight." Rickard glanced at his watch. "That must be him at the door now."

In a few moments he was leading into the room a bewildered, cunning-looking creature.

"Allow me to introduce Vernon Dixley," Rickard announced, "a rat in human guise. Y'know, I'm not so sure he doesn't look better in a mask."

Dixley cringed in the corner, a rat with that animal's courage in an emergency. "Why have you brought me here?" he whined.

Rickard explained. "Not only have we retrieved your documents, my friend, but you're going to refund all the money you've been paid."

"I—I have none left," Dixley stammered.

"Not now, you haven't, Rickard agreed. "I've taken it all from your safe." He went back to his briefcase and took out the cash. "Here you are—five hundred pounds for you, colonel, fifteen hundred for you, Webbley..."

The distribution went on.

At length Rickard glanced at his watch again. "And now, gentlemen, I will throw Dixley, the hound, to the wolves. You, Evans, will probably want to chance your arm.

"But I suggest you all go out into the alleyway. This house isn't mine, and the owner usually comes in at nine thirty. As you know, gentlemen, I am useful at unpicking a lock."

The Black Bag

At eight-thirty Villiers was cracking open a safe. At nine-thirty he was cracking open a head.

The safe belonged to Colonel Carthage, who was entertaining in the lounge of his home whilst Villiers was in the library, pocketing the Carthage Diamonds.

The head in question belonged to Uriah Catchpenny, licensed pawnbroker and unlicensed fence.

Villiers went direct from the colonel's west end flat to the jeweller's east end hovel; and a coded rat-tat admitted him to Catchpenny's private parlour. Curtly, Villiers laid his haul on the table. "How much, Shylock?"

The old man examined the diamonds with professional scepticism; but the uncontrolled rubbing of palms testified to his approval. "2,000."

"I'm no jewel expert," Villiers snapped. "But I can read. *The Gazette* says they're worth 50 grand."

Catchpenny shrugged. "Then I suggest you sell them to the editor of *The Gazette*."

"You win," Villiers grunted, his remorseless eyes following like a spotlight as the old man shuffled over to the bureau and dragged out the black Gladstone bag. *Dragged* out, not lifted. It was crammed with notes tonight. So Villiers vaulted the table and grabbed the bag. "Hand over, you chiselling skinflint."

Fearing to lose all that beautiful money, the old man screamed: "Help… Polisssssss…."

The cry fizzled out; and so did Catchpenny's life, as Villiers coshed the jeweller scientifically behind the ear.

A police whistle was sounding outside.

An icicle of fear caressed Villiers' spine. To his long list to crimes could be added a murder rap. He crammed the cash from the Gladstone bag into his overcoat pockets, and slid out into the night.

On the pavement he bumped into his arch-enemy, P.C. Dawkins; but at the instant of impact the constable had one hand engaged in the performance of his whistle solo, and so Villiers avoided capture. Like a startled rabbit he bolted through the warren of streets that led to the fringe of the city, and within twenty minutes had gone to earth—sipping whisky in the Bishop's flat above a block of offices.

The Bishop had no ecclesiastical claim to the nickname; a pontifical demeanour alone had earned him the title. He was an insurance broker—to the commercial world by day, to the underworld by night. His dealings embraced all the risks of criminal catastrophe.

Villiers was saying: "My premiums are up to date. I want protection."

The Bishop nodded. "A free passport, perhaps?"

"More. A new identity—a face the cops can't recognise. They're after me, I'm telling you, and Heaven knows what fingerprints I've left at the scene of the—"

"Of the murder?" the Bishop prompted, sampling the words with relish. "Sure, I'll get Surge to fix you a facial" (After blotting his professional copy-book, Surge had turned to black market doctoring; a modern Aladdin's genie, giving new faces for old.)

* * * * * *

Undergoing his facial the next day, Villiers was dreaming dreams—a confused canvas of coshes, conscience, and cops. But looming large in the picture was the jeweller's black Gladstone bag. And the first thing Villiers noticed, on coming out of the anesthetic, was the surgeon's black bag: it might have been the twin to the murder bag. He shuddered, trying not to see an omen in this....

After some months, the new Villiers emerged to meet and cheat the world with the aid of the measly hundred pounds the Bishop had given him. He steered clear of safe-breaking for a while: his last encounter had sapped his nerve. He dabbled in confidence trickery for a bit, but found that even he had lost confidence in himself.

The twin shadow of the two bags followed him everywhere—a shadow that refused to disappear at sundown.

Came the time when he had invested his last three-penny piece on a cup of tea, and was sitting dejectedly in the café, casting a speculative eye on the cash register. And then the blaring radio was suddenly hushed, and the announcer read a message that was to revolutionise Villiers' fortune:

"Will Derek Carstone, last heard of five years ago in London, go to Dalebury Hospital, where his father is dangerously ill."

In his 30 years, Villiers had enjoyed as many aliases, but it was as Derek Carstone that he was on nodding terms with the Registrar of Births and Deaths. His father, a wealthy businessman, had made his shrewdest move in kicking out the black sheep five years ago.

Villiers smiled grimly. He would go at once to Dalebury; not to the hospital, but to his old home, where there was a bulging safe—one he had never dared to crack while his father was about.

The old homestead was in darkness that evening as Villiers entered through the window. But he hardly needed the aid of a torch to tread the familiar passages that led to the library. This job was far easier than shooting at a sitting bird!

There was a cocktail cabinet close to the safe, and by the light of his torch Villiers mixed himself a drink. He proposed a silent toast to success.

But the liquid never touched his lips, for at that moment the room was flooded with light, and a large policeman stood framed in the doorway. With the constable was Villiers' mother—the only relative who still retained an affection for the black sheep of the family.

His mother said: "That's the man I saw breaking in, officer. I'll leave him to you while I dash off to the hospital."

Villiers thought quickly. "Why, mother, I'm coming with you. I got the radio message." Seeing the blank stare on his mother's face, Villiers looked wildly about the room and pointed to his photograph. "That's me. Your son!" he said hysterically.

"I know the voice," said his mother, *"but I don't recognise the face."*

The policeman studied the photograph keenly. "If you're that man, sir, there are some questions I want to ask you."

Last heard of... Villiers had a date with the hangman and an introduction to a different kind of black bag.

The Brimstone Story

Ladies and gentlemen (said Humphrey Merridon, the managing director)...

I am often asked the recipe for success. On the occasion of my retirement, perhaps the time is now opportune to pass on my recipe:

Let me take you back some 50 years to when, as an insignificant stripling of fifteen, I was completing my education at Dr. Bavistock's Academy for Honest Young Gentlemen.

Now some scholars revel in the perpetual society of their kind, whilst others do not. I was a non-reveller. A timorous bookworm with a deficiency of muscle and a surplus of inhibition, I had spent six socially-misfit years at Bavistock Academy.

Mark you, I should have been no better off at home, for my father was a tyrant and a waster, doing his best to ruin a steady family business.

A word about Mr. Wilbrahim Bavistock, my mentor. An awesome character, Bavistock. Tall, broad-shouldered, bushy-bearded, I regarded him as a cross between the prophet Elijah and W.G Grace; and he wielded a cane as skillfully as Grace ever wielded a bat. There was a difference, however. Bavistock's beard was of a fiery ginger hue, and he had a cast in his right eye.

What a teacher! And what a preacher! Standing on the dais in Main Hall, the whole school assembly before him, he would switch from Euclid's theorems to the Life Hereafter with eloquent facility. Hell-fire and brimstone, he preached, flourishing his cane baton-wise as though conducting a heavenly orchestration.

At the end of his peroration, he would thunder: "Hands up, the miserable sinners!" Invariably, my hand would rise in company with many others. Bavistock would then descend to the body of the hall and cane the outstretched hands. If I was quick enough, I would take advantage of his wonky eye and quickly withdraw my hand. There was some merit, I thought, to being a happy sinner.

In this my last year at the Academy, my future was in the melting-pot. My wastrel father had ordained me to win a scholarship, thus to complete my education at College at no charge to himself, then eventually to take over the family business. Father made it sound so simple—but there happened to be 49 other candidates, with the will to win and the spur of personal reward. The only reward my father offered was the negative one of a sound thrashing if I failed.

Ladies and gentlemen, I confess I was a miserable sinner. The fear of failure, with the thrashing to follow, transformed me into a cheat.

I had only one real friend at the Academy—Radley Major. He one of those bright lights who shine in all directions: cricket, football, athletics and, of course, scholarship.

"Look here, Merridon," he said to me one day. "I'm in no hurry to go to college. I've got a corking idea! I'll win the scholarship next year, and help you win it this year!"

And so in due course the corking idea was bottled into practice. Radley sat directly beside me at the examination table; and to facilitate my copy-work he wrote in a large copper-plate. As an added precaution, I had fixed magnifying discs to my spectacles, and the rest was easy.

After the examination I was once more a comparatively happy creature—until a new and more intangible fear came to replace the fear of a good thrashing. Just at that time Dr. Bavistock chose to launch an intensive "Hell-fire and brimstone" campaign. As was his custom, he assembled us in Main Hall after our Friday afternoon P.T. session: physical jerks followed by spiritual jerks. Thus perspiring bodily, we were in a malleable mood to perspire soulfully.

"Oh, thou collection of disobedient heathens," Bavistock began, and he proceeded to expound the Ten Commandments.

I was largely unmoved by these strictures, but my conscience anticipated an eleventh commandment: "Thou shalt not cheat." Relief at its absence was short-lived, however, for the reverent doctor returned to the First Commandment and elaborated on them all, in turn.

"Thou shalt not steal.... Now, boys, that doesn't simply forbid you to put your hand into your neighbour's pocket and extract a penny-piece. You may steal by false representation by *cheating*."

Allowing for his wonky eye, I'm sure the doctor brandished his cane directly at me as he spoke; and when the invitation came for miserable sinners to put their hands up, my palm was the first respondent....

I knew little peace of mind in the days preceding the announcement of examination results. Or nights. One frequent nightmare placed me in the middle of the football field, heading goalwards. The goalkeeper (old Jonks, the school porter) was lighting a bonfire in the goal mouth.

As I approached, Jonks would scoop me up with a giant shovel and consign me to the flames. Dr. Bavistock (the referee) would snatch the football from my toes—the ball promptly exploding into a ball of brimstone, to be poured on my charred head....

Little wonder, ladies and gentlemen, that I began to hope that I had failed the scholarship. At long last, we were assembled in Main Hall to hear the results. Bavistock prolonged the agony of suspense by starting from the bottom of the list:

Fiftieth, Dobson, G.H.—12 per cent of total marks. Wretched Boy!

"Forty-ninth, Johnson, N.C.—20 percent. Ignoramus!"

And so on—and upwards.

Cheats never prosper! I, Merridon, H.W., was placed at the top of the list, with 95 per cent. The applause rang in my ears like the hollow laughter of all the devils in Hell.

I could stand no more. Directly after the ceremony I went along to the Headmaster's study, so briskly that I omitted to place the Atlas of all Nations strategically in the seat of my trousers.

"Come in!" thundered the doctor. His stern expression melted to a wintry smile, however, when he saw it was his number one scholar. "Yes, Merridon, my boy, what is it?"

"P-Please," I stammered, "I don't like the brimstone and treacle."

"Brimstone and *treacle*, boy? Who authorized the Matron to serve brimstone and treacle?"

"Oh, no, sir, I mean Hell-fire and brimstone, sir…." And so the whole sorry story came out.

Old Baverstock came up trumps. Instead of caning me, he stretched out his arms like a patriarch in benediction. The punishment was purely crime-fitting. Marks were deducted for those subjects in which I had cheated, and I slid thankfully down to fourth place. An honest failure….

Home for the holidays. I got my thrashing all right but somehow it didn't seem to matter any more.

And of course I had to start work straight away—but not in my father's business. You see, he had wagered heavily that I would win the scholarship, and he had to sell up his business to meet the wager.

So I started as messenger boy in this firm. The rest was hard work, and a great deal of private study, combined with the evergreen memory of my bitter experience.

In conclusion, ladies and gentlemen, I could do worse than recommend you to an honest-to-goodness dose of Bavistock's Fire and Brimstone. And, who knows? You may scoop in a little of the treacle on the way.

The Copper for the Guy

Police Sergeant Devons was always ready to mix pleasure with business when occasion permitted. So he came to be leaning on the wall bordering Mr. Saxon's back yard this fine November evening, an unobtrusive spectator of a magnificent fireworks display.

Saxon, the grocer, normally a short-tempered, crochety individual, was in fine fettle tonight. He was letting off fireworks with machine-gun rapidity, and he had lit a mammoth bonfire in the centre of his cobbled yard. At Saxon's invitation, a horde of cheering youngsters was feeding home-made effigies of Guy Fawkes to the hungry flames.

Sergeant Devons smiled as he saw Billy Bates place his guy on the bonfire. He noted how carefully Septimus Saxon assisted the lad to do so. The policeman had been introduced to the guy only that morning. His thoughts flashed back to the scene.

Billy Bates was the village terror with cheek enough to ask the police sergeant to spare a copper for the guy. The effigy had been a worthy specimen, clad in an old trilby hat and a raincoat. It had stood ramrod-backed on the pavement close to Saxon's shop.

"Seeking the alms of the law, eh, Billy?" Devons had jested. "Well, seeing as it's the Fifth today—here, buy yourself some fireworks."

"Thank you, Mister." At the sight of the sergeant's shilling, the lad had prattled merrily on. "I've only just made the guy; got up jolly early to do it. There's a guy competition at Gregger's toyshop this afternoon."

"I know," the sergeant had replied. "Mr. Gregger has asked me to judge the guys."

"Then this evening," the lad had continued, "I'm taking it to the fireworks display in Mr. Saxon's yard. When he invited me just now he must have forgotten that I put a football through his window!"

Devons had nodded genially and strolled on to the police station, to receive the daily crime report from Constable Hawkey.

"Morning, Sarge. Mr. Saxon's been in to withdraw his charge against Billy Bates, of Wilful Damage to property—to wit, one plate-glass window—and to return the football that did it!"

"So I hear," Devons had replied. "I wonder, now, do I detect the milk of human kindness *or the poison of ulterior motive?*"

"Farmer Benwood has been in too," the constable had continued, "to report the theft of a scarecrow. It appears the scarecrow was wearing a raincoat."

"A raincoated scarecrow, eh?" Devons had replied, musingly.

His thoughts had been halted by the ringing of a telephone.

The call had come from the police station at Lower Midgely, which was separated from Upper Midgely by Farmer Benwood's stretch of lands.

"Sergeant Devons?" queried the caller. "There's been a murder. Old Sammy Wicks, the moneylender. Head bashed in. Seems half the tradesmen in your district could be suspects."

Thereafter had followed for Sergeant Devons one of those hectic days. But he had still found time to judge the guys at Gregger's toyshop in the afternoon.

And he had the time, now, to be standing against the wall of Saxon's back yard, watching the magnificent fireworks display.

It wasn't until the final squib had been exploded, and the bonfire was but an ashen glow, that Devons made his presence known. "Good evening, Mr. Saxon. Nice little show you put on."

The grocer looked up with a start. "Why, good evening, Sergeant. Won't you come in for a chat? The kettle's on the boil and the missus is away."

Readily enough Devons made his way round to the front door and was ushered into the cosy kitchen.

As he handed his visitor a cup of tea, Saxon asked casually: "Any news of poor old Sammy Wix's murderer?"

"I've made no arrest as yet," the sergeant replied modestly. "But I have a theory."

"Which I'd very much like to hear."

"Yes, Mr. Saxon. Yes, I dare say you would. So I'll tell you. But I'll play safe on names. Say the murderer was—"

"Say it was me!" Saxon suggested. "For the sake of argument."

"All right," said Devons. "I won't argue. Say it was you. This is how the theory goes:

"You, in common with other Upper Midgely tradesmen, owed Sammy Wix money. Last night you called on him to ask for time to pay, but he refused. In the heat of the moment you picked up the poker and struck the poor old devil. There was a struggle so you struck, and struck again.

"Leaving Sammy dead on the carpet, and stopping only to wipe your fingerprints from the poker, you rushed from the scene."

"This is all very interesting, Sergeant," Saxon said. "Care for another cup of tea?"

"Thank you, Mr. Saxon. Now where was I? Or rather, where were you? Ah yes, in Farmer Benwood's fields, which you had to cross to get back to Upper Midgely. At this point, Saxon, you spotted the bloodstain on your raincoat.

"Panic-stricken—for I'll say this about you, you're not a habitual murderer—you looked wildly about.

"It was a stroke of luck, you thought, seeing a scarecrow wearing a raincoat. It was a simple matter to swap your coat for the one the scarecrow was wearing.

"But in the calm light of morning, you realised that the coat out there in the fields, presented damning evidence. So you decided to retrieve it.

"Unfortunately, Billy Bates was astir before you; he had already pinched the scarecrow—raincoat an' all—to make his guy. In fact he was displaying the guy on the pavement close to your shop.

"Your problem was how to retrieve the coat without arousing the lad's suspicions. You solved it with a brilliant inspiration. You invited the lad to a fireworks display, which in no other circumstances would a Scrooge like you, Saxon, have arranged. And, of course, you withdrew the charge of window-breaking so as to gain the lad's confidence."

The sergeant drained his tea with relish. "How's that for a theory, Mr. Saxon?"

Saxon drained his tea with equal relish. "A pretty theory, Sergeant, but one hardly likely to hold up in court. As you yourself admit, the fingerprints were wiped from the poker. As for the raincoat, you must have been watching while I burned the guy. That bloodstain will take a lot of finding!"

Devons placed his cup carefully on the table, and said slowly: "I was round at Gregger's toyshop this afternoon, judging guys. I took the opportunity to swap the scarecrow-guy's raincoat for another of a similar pattern. The bloodstained coat, now at the police laboratory, will give me all the evidence I need. You burned the wrong coat!"

There was a crashing of china as Saxon's cup fell to the floor from nerveless fingers.

The Eternal Quadrangle

The doorbell shrilled, striking a discordant note on the quiet little party spirit.

"I'll go," Gordon Haverlon said. "You carry on with the game, Beryl."

Instinct warned him that his wedding anniversary was to be ruined, and when he opened the front door his fears were confirmed. On the doorstep stood handsome Stephen Voxley, as debonair as ever—and as devilish.

"Hello, stranger," Voxley said with a mocking grin. "It seems ages since we met in Cairo."

"For all I care," Gordon blazed, "you can go right back there!"

Voxley shrugged his broad shoulders. "The first thing I hear on my return to England," he said, "Is that you're married. I'd like to meet the second Mrs. Haverlon. *So would the first Mrs. Haverlon.*"

Scenting blackmail, Gordon wondered how much he would need to raise on his cosy semi-detached house. Never a double-talker, he came straight to the point. "What price your silence?"

Stephen Voxley replied airily, "I don't want your cash—I'm going back to Cairo soon, to pull off a big deal in Army surplus."

Gordon was bewildered. "What else d'you want?"

"Simply your company, old man. Put me up for a few days. I hear your new wife is a good-looker!"

Gordon clenched his fist, itching to flatten his visitor's classic nose. Instead, he led the tormentor into the hall and helped him off with his coat. As he did so, he asked casually, "How's Nimra?"

Voxley sniggered. "The Arab bint?" Then—with mock apology—"Sorry, Gordon, that's no way to speak of your *lawful* wedded wife."

"Quiet, man," Gordon pleaded, pointing towards the lounge doors. In a muttered whisper he went on, "I lost all feeling for Nimra when she ran off with you, Voxley, but I did wonder how she was getting on."

Voxley replied callously, "I don't happen to know—or care. You see, I've deserted her."

"I might have guessed it," Gordon growled. "Well, you'd better come right in."

He introduced his guest as a business friend. "A very close friend," he added. (This would prepare Beryl for a lodger on her hands.)

Beryl greeted Voxley with her natural charm, and Gordon was alarmed to see the reaction. The return handshake was almost a caress.

Now Voxley took the stage. "Good evening all," he beamed. "So you're having a jolly celebration. Now I know some good games."

Gordon sidled into a corner seat, an outsider at his own party. The evening, which had been flying on carefree wings, dragged on braked wheels.

He got little sleep that night. The malignancy of the guest in the spare bedroom penetrated throughout the house. Bitterly, Gordon regretted the day he had first met Voxley....

Five years ago, Gordon had been sent out by his firm to keep an eye on their Cairo branch. He hadn't been overworked, and the evenings were lonely. So he had been glad to scrape acquaintance with Voxley, who hid his true light under a bushel of charm.

Voxley conducted a shady enterprise from a shabby back street office, and employed a pretty secretary, Nimra Bint Taher Ezreem.

"Tigress," the name Nimra meant. Gordon, who married the flighty Arab girl, had never been able to tame her. After a few tempestuous weeks, the tigress drew her claws and lacerated the marriage, by running off with Voxley.

Shortly afterwards Gordon had returned to England. Nimra having forfeited a claim on him, he had wiped the memory-slate clean. A year ago he had gone through a form of marriage with Beryl, and it had been a genuine love match.

But now history was repeating itself. Voxley, the universal heart-throb, had come to rob him of his second "wife."

Gordon saw himself as the loser either way. If he sent the cad packing, Voxley would blab to the police, and to Beryl. If he let the blackmailer stay, Beryl might fall to his charms.

Gordon tossed and turned, but sleep wouldn't come. So he lit a cigarette. The flame illuminated the peacefully sleeping form beside him—the serene expression on the heart-shaped face, the soft brown waves which cascaded over the wide, firm brow, the gentle half-smile which sleep failed to erase.

He yearned for the same serenity, and was tempted to wake Beryl and to confess the whole story. But was it fair to involve her in the intrigue? In any case, he was so afraid of losing her that he dared not risk her reaction to the news.

Instead, he lit another cigarette… then another.

With the fifth smoke, inspiration came. A wild, wonderful plan of counter-attack.

A few days later—air-bound for Cairo—Gordon was putting the plan into action. He proposed to blackmail the blackmailer! And the best way to do it, he thought, was to snoop around Voxley's Cairo office and unearth the shady secrets tucked away in the files.

And the person to help reveal those secrets? Why, his real wife Nimra—who had been Voxley's secretary. Seeing that Voxley had deserted her, the spitfire would seize this opportunity of revenge!

As the plane winged eastwards, Gordon's feelings were a mixture of elation and despair.

Elation, because Mr. Williams, his general manager, had readily agreed to Gordon paying a flying visit to Cairo. That branch was not doing too well.

Elation, also, because Beryl had believed his story of a business trip to Birmingham.

Elation, because Voxley had believed him too, and had promised to move out to the local inn, until Gordon returned.

Despair arose from the big question mark: *How long would Voxley stay at the inn?* It was a chance Gordon had to take. He tried to shake off his doubts; the prospect of failure was too shattering to contemplate.

When the plane landed, events took a sudden and surprising turn. And, in the turning, Gordon was given an alternative blackmail weapon. A more certain weapon, that would save him the trouble of snooping in Voxley's office, and save the embarrassment of meeting Nimra.

In the airport canteen, Gordon saw Nimra's brother Fazeer. When he had last seen Fazeer, the giant Arab had been managing a curio chop in the bazaar. Now he was a white-robed, red-sashed waiter!

Gordon did not go up to his brother-in-law, but spoke to another Arab waiter with whom he had once had some acquaintance.

"Tell me, Sayed, why is Fazeer Ibin Taher Ezreem, the shopkeeper, working here?"

Sayed grinned. "He work here so he can watch every aeroplane come in. He have dagger in cloak. He after blood of Engleezi."

"Which Engleezi?" Gordon asked excitedly.

"The Engleesh Meester Voxley. He is the one who ran away from Fazeer's seester, Nimra."

Here then was the wonderful blackmail opportunity, as Gordon saw it. He could now return to England and order Voxley out of the house, neck and crop. If Voxley refused to go, Gordon would threaten to put Fazeer on the blackmailer's trail. The cowardly Voxley valued his skin more highly even than the chance of an affair. He would be off like a shot.

The decision made, Gordon went to book an air passage home, allowing himself 48 hours to clear up the inspection of the Cairo branch.

"Sorry, sir," said the booking clerk. "I haven't a seat for another week."

Gordon's pleading, cajolery, and hints of bribery were all in vain. The sympathetic clerk could do nothing. Once again despair tempered elation. It was Voxley's constant boast that he could make any conquest within a week.

Seven days; 168 hours; thousands of minutes; countless seconds, that staggered when they should have ticked....

To take his mind off what might be happening at home Gordon spent most of the time at the Cairo office. Working, waiting, snatching a little sleep, and more working.

At the end of the week—haggard, unkempt, and tense to breaking point—Gordon went to the airport. His plane was not due to leave for half an hour, so he entered the canteen.

He thought at first his tortured mind was playing tricks. That Voxley was standing at the end of the counter... linked arm in arm with a girl, whose back was turned.

When the man he thought was Voxley said: "I'll get you a cup of tea, Beryl, darling," Gordon knew it wasn't a hallucination. It was a grim fact.... It was the end.

In a sudden burst of anger, Gordon slipped behind the counter, to tell the vengeful Arab waiter that his prey was within dagger's distance.

But anger quickly subsided. When Fazeer Ezreem greeted him, Gordon's reply was listless and conventional. "*Keef Harlak*? (How are you?)" he asked Fazeer. "And how is Nimra?"

Fazeer told Gordon how he was, and how Nimra was. The news made Gordon whistle.

Then Fazeer spotted Voxley. With a wild triumphant cry, the Arab leaped the counter. The place was in a pandemonium, as excited Orientals jostled for a grandstand view.

Voxley saw Fazeer and, pushing Beryl aside, he ran for his life.

Gordon sat on a couch in the corner of the lounge and pondered on the might-have-been, especially bearing in mind Fazeer's news which had caused the whistle.

A silvery voice asked: "May I join you? I won't ask why you're in Cairo when you're supposed to be in Birmingham."

Gordon replied bitterly, "I won't ask why *you're* here, Beryl."

"Then I'll tell you." Beryl gave Gordon's arm an affectionate squeeze. "I pretended to fall in love with Stephen Voxley. And I persuaded him to tell me the secret hold he had over you."

Gordon, haggard no longer, said: "How did you know there was a secret?"

"Firstly, because you introduced Voxley as a close friend—yet you'd never even mentioned him before. And I knew you had something on your mind when I found five cigarette stubs on the bedside table!"

Hope dawning, Gordon said: "And now that you know the worst?"

"I came to Cairo to talk things over with your real wife. But whatever Nimra says, I shall stay with you."

Gordon smiled, the first time for many days. "That Arab you saw chasing Voxley," he said, "is avenging his sister Nimra. Fazeer tells me that because Voxley deserted her, Nimra committed suicide...."

Gordon embraced Beryl.

"Darling," he said, "will you marry me?"

The Play's the Thing

Ever since he had played Julius Caesar in the village pageant, Bob Drake had lived in a daydream world of greasepaint and encores. His every action had become theatrical, sometimes to the point of lunatic, and his soulful rendering of "Time, gentlemen, please" in the Pitchfork and Wheelbarrow was a daily source of delight to prosaic sons of the soil.

Drake didn't cast himself as a juvenile lead—eighteen stone took some camouflaging—but for character stuff he was the answer to a casting director's prayer. He would tell you so himself.

When Super Kolossal Films Inc. pitched their studios on the borders of Mudbury Molton, Drake was confident that a word in the right direction would bring about his early retirement from inn-keeping.

Witness him one evening, wielding the beer-pumps with dramatic flourish before a gallery of gaping throats. "To be or not to be? That is the question."

"To be," replied Farmer Watson. "Another pint of brown ale."

Hardly had the laughter subsided when old Adam Laxton entered the pub, waving a slip of paper aloft, to rob Drake of the limelight. "A letter from Lunnen," the centenarian cackled. "I'm famous after a hunnerd year!"

Bob Drake quickly took the letter, read it suspiciously, and grudgingly announced: "It's right enough, the *Daily Globe* are sending a man down to interview Adam."

Amid a hubbub of congratulation, a shrewd voice yelled: "Drinks all round!"

Drake gave the signal. "Right, lads, it's on the house; but keep it reasonable." He pushed a foaming mug into the hands of the centenarian, who tottered gleefully back to his favourite corner seat.

After a moment's thought, Drake made a speech: "Friends, Romans, countrymen. This interview is an honour, not only for Adam Laxton but for the whole village. But you may well ask, is he the man to see it through? A good old sort is Adam, but we all know he's a gormless old dodderer. Why not select a younger man to impersonate him for the occasion?"

There was a murmur of assent. "What about young Ephraim?" someone suggested. Young Ephraim was Adam's 80-year-old son.

"Not likely," said another. "Ephraim's gormlesser than his dad!"

"What I had in mind," Drake explained, "was a middle-aged man suitably disguised. In other words, an actor. And there's only one man can do it."

Farmer Watson shook his head. "I doubt very much whether we can get Sir Laurence."

"A local actor," Bob added hastily. "To wit, me."

"I'll second that motion," said Bill Crump, who had the biggest ale slate account at the Pitchfork and Wheelbarrow, "and mine's a brown alc."

"I'll third it," said another with his eye on the chalk column.

Bob Drake, with his eye on the cash register, declared, "I don't need a seconder, thank 'ee, or a thirder. We'll take the motion as carried, and it only remains to settle it with old Adam."

The centenarian, who, being hard of hearing was under the impression that toasting operations were still in progress, beamed broadly at the mention of his name. So Drake explained the situation as tactfully as one could in a voice that would have reached the back of the Palladium. "And in exchange for your consent, Adam," he concluded, "there's a free pint of beer a day, for a month. What d'you say?"

"Pint, please," said Adam briefly.

Now, in making the proposal, Bob Drake had not so much the good of the village at heart as the good of Bob Drake. A successful impersonation should convince Super Kolossal Films they had a born actor on their doorstep. And were they not seeking talent for their new picture?

The film in question featured Danny "The Cherub" Langland. It was a school story set to a sports field background, and at judicious intervals in the lad's life his father appeared to ladle out doses of good advice.

Unknown to the film moguls, Drake had earmarked for himself the part of the Cherub's father. He had even scripted the major scene—heavy handed similes on the theme that life was a game of cricket. The newspaper interview would give Bob the chance to give his script an airing.

During the coming week Drake prepared for the masquerade as earnestly as a Hollywood star on an Oscar hunt.

He went up to town to select his greasepaint and artificial wrinkles, and then from the vicar he borrowed a flowing beard that had once graced a stage Methuselah.

On the eventful day, Drake went round to Adam Laxton's house to await the reporter. He got the centenarian safely out of the way by dispatching that worthy, whose thirst the ages had not dimmed, to the Pitchfork and Wheelbarrow, where the morning session was under the presidency of the barmaid.

"Good morning, Mr. Laxton," the reporter greeted Drake, adding involuntarily, "Good gracious, Mr. Laxton! I should have thought you were nearer 200 years old."

"Ar, I had a bit of a late night," Bob replied. "Celebrating, you know."

With one hand he proffered a chair to his visitor. With the other he denuded his brow of 100 years' worth of wrinkles.

"And to what, sir, do you attribute your longevity?"

With an effort, Drake transferred his voice to the upper register. "Dang it, man, to have been born so long ago."

"Do you drink?"

"As a matter of fact," Drake replied with misleading truthfulness, "I never buy the stuff."

"What are your views on life, Mr. Laxton?"

Ah! This was the clue Drake was seeking. Eagerly, he consulted his own notebook, and began to read in the approved in-town-tonight manner: "Life is like a game of cricket, I always think."

"Or like a game of football," suggested the reporter. "We all have a goal to aim at."

"Take cricket," Drake insisted. "Life is but an innings; for some of short duration; for others a lengthy spell at the crease. Speaking personally, like, I've made 100 and I'm still not out."

"Then there's golf, Mr. Laxton."

"Cricket," Drake said, firmly, "is like life. Play a straight bat and you won't get caught out."

He went on to elaborate the theme. How well all this would sound in the film—particularly for the pep talk with the wayward Cherub in that scene following the cricket match.

At length, he ushered out the reporter before the issue was confused with similes on basketball and throwing the discus. Cricket, he insisted, was the theme of the interview, not the Olympic Games.

The Globe turned up trumps. Drake's philosophy was printed in full, with the accent on his words of Wisden wisdom. On the day of publication Drake travelled to London, returning with a bundle of newspapers to distribute amongst his favourite customers.

One copy he enclosed with a letter to Super Kolossal Films. He admitted his innocent deception, but pointed out that the masquerade proved his acting ability, so how about the part of the Cherub's father?

Until the reply came he found himself constantly repeating—but now with personal application—"To be, or not to be?"

When the reply did come, an exultant Drake waved the letter before his customers at the bar. "To be!" he exclaimed. "I'm to call at the studios tomorrow to discuss the part." The cheering which followed, and the rendering of "For he's a jolly good fellow," were obvious forerunners to the invitation, "Drinks all round, lads."

*   *   *   *   *   *

Dawn had hardly cracked the next day when Bob Drake presented himself at the studio gates. After a delay that to his stage-stricken mind felt like eons, the gates were opened and the wheels of cinematography began turning. He followed those wheels around in a seemingly endless procession. Make-up tests, camera tests, script conferences, the whole works. He was bandied about from one official to another; although pending the arrival of the casting director, nobody seemed to know exactly why Drake was there.

Exciting though this round of activity might be, Drake could hardly contain himself for the interview with the casting director, so anxious was he to sign on the dotted line which led to stardom.

The director appeared at last. "How d'you do, Mr. Drake?" he greeted the stage-struck publican.

"How d'you do, Mr. Super Kolossal?"

"No, the name's Goldheimer. Now, Mr. Drake, about this role—"

"Yes!" Drake said eagerly.

"Unfortunately, the part of the father is already cast. But in view of your authoritative remarks on the game..." The director paused, looking down at the script.

"Yes, yes?"

"I am going to offer you a ten-second cameo role, filmed long-distance, from the boundary. You can be the umpire of the school cricket match!"

The Proposal

The twin personal-column notices stood out in the pages of the sober *Daily Times* like jesters at a funeral.

The first, under Box No. 59, read: *I would like to hear from the esteemed gentleman answering to the name of Roger Barslowe, Esq., who lived at 9 Elm Lane, Darchester, some 15-odd years ago. If he will kindly contact me, he will learn something to his advantage—or mebbe disadvantage, I can't rightly say which.*

Under Box No. 59A, the advertiser requested a good lady answering to the name of Miss Amelia Shelgrade to learn something to *her* advantage (or mebbe disadvantage).

A week later, Roger Barslowe drove up to a cottage in Darchester. In typically carefree fashion he slammed the door of the car which belonged to the firm for which he sold cosmetics, and rapped on the cottage door.

Roger had sold most things in the course of a light-hearted career, from millinery to soap detergents; but this call was commercially off the record. He was here at the invitation of Box No. 59, now identified as Joshua Radwick.

Joshua was a silvery-haired old man, with a back bent by the weight of some eighty years and the hazards of his former occupation. He had been a postman.

His weather-beaten face was clouded, as by some secret depression. "Do come into the parlour," he said solemnly. "I'll make a cup of tea as soon as Miss Amelia Shelgrade arrives."

Roger was intrigued. "So you've located Box No. 59A too?"

"Right enough, sir. And I thought it best to have you both together, to explain things personal-like. Do sit down on the sofa."

Roger hardly had time to ponder the mystery further before he was on his feet to greet his fellow visitor.

Amelia Shelgrade, like himself, was approaching 40, but here the resemblance ended. She was a vinegary spinster of doleful aspect and her temperament had obviously been cramped by sitting on the shelf for so long.

However, she did brighten up a little at the sight of Roger's good looks, as if recognising a potential ladder to step off the shelf; and she sat alone beside him on the settee.

Joshua handed round the tea cups. "Now I must explain why I brought you here—"

"Yes, you must," Amelia snapped.

"Take your time, grand-dad," Roger said. "I like a good mystery."

With a quiver in his voice, the old man began: "First, I must take you back fifteen years, when you were living in your respective residences in Elm Lane. I was the postman in them days, about to retire on pension.

"Me last day on duty it was, which by custom should be taken easy. But was it? Oh no, they wanted me to do an extra round, on behalf of Jim Huggins, what was sick."

Joshua's face burned, as if reviving some of the anger he had felt at the time. "I was livid inside of me. You see, I had properly resigned myself to not having another stroke of work to do in me natural.

"It didn't help none when they gave me a gold watch. 'For 50 years devoted service,' they had wrote on it.

"Devoted service? Huh! What with blisters in the summer, and chilblains in the winter, I hated every minute of it.

"Anyhow, I took the bag and set off on me round. It was a long trek and by the time I got to Elm Lane I was fair whacked. No. 9 and No. 155 there were letters for—at opposite ends of the lane.

"Suddenly something came over me... and I slipped the letters in me pocket."

The old man paused to sip his tea, with shaking hands, and Roger smiled at Amelia.

But the lady was not amused. She sat upright, prim and proper, bleak and bitter. Like a senna pod plant, Roger thought.

"Soon aftewr that," Joshua continued, "I was took ill, and what with being in and out of hospital like a jack-in-the-box I forgot about the letters. And when I did remember 'em, darned if I could recall where I had put 'em.

"Howsoever, I'm thankful to say I did come across them last week. I called at the two houses and found you had both moved. So I ups and puts them adverts in the *Daily Times*. Cost me a week's pension, it did, but it was worth it to ease me conscience."

"You shouldn't have done that," Roger said.

"Oh yes he should," Amelia snapped. "Where are the letters?"

"Here's yours, ma'am." Joshua handed her a square, pastel-blue envelope which exuded a scent of stale lavender.

At the sight of the envelope Amelia murmured, "From Victor." She snatched the letter from the old man's grasp and read the contents avidly.

Then she fastened a grim gaze on the old man's troubled face. "You monster. You—you criminal. This is a proposal of marriage. In the absence of a reply, Victor says he is going away." She added tearfully, "How can I reply fifteen years later?"

To hide the old man's embarrassment, Roger hastily opened his own envelope and read the contents.

He burst into laughter. "At least it's not a double tragedy, grand-dad. In fact, you've saved me ten pounds. This is a bill from my wine merchants."

Joshua looked happier. "I'm glad of that anyway, sir."

Amelia dabbed her eyes with a lace-bordered handkerchief. "What about my single tragedy?" she whispered.

Roger carried on his role of peacemaker. "If you care to accept a lift to the station, Miss Shelgrade, there's something I'd like to say to you in secret. You may find that it need not be a tragedy after all!"

The lady brightened up considerably, and Joshua smiled for the first time.

In the car, Amelia snuggled close to Roger. He said nothing. They reached the station all too soon, and Amelia asked anxiously, "Was there not something you had to say to me?"

"Yes, Miss Shelgrade. If you insist. I was going to say that there was no need for you to have hurt that old man's feelings. It couldn't have brought back the past—even if your proposal story had been true."

"What do you mean?" Amelia asked faintly. "If it had been true?"

"I mean you were simply treating us to an exhibition of inhibition. The only romance about that letter was the romance of your silly little mind."

"How dare you say that!"

"Fifteen years ago," Roger continued relentlessly, "Victor was the Darchester milliner. Happily married at that. I happen to know because I sold hats for him. I expect that letter was simply an invoice or something of the sort. Victor always sent out his bills on scented paper. Am I right, Miss Shelgrade?"

In reply, Amelia got out of the car, tore up the letter and threw the pieces into the air. And Roger knew he was right.

He whistled cheerily and prepared to drive away. But first he brought out his own letter, and read it again. A proposal, if ever there was one, he thought.

Dear Mr. Barslowe (wrote the wine merchants)—*We propose to offer you the post of U.K. Sales Manager, provided you commence straight away.*

Roger tore up the letter, shrugged his shoulders, and drove away.

The Way to the Town Hall

In the waiting-room adjoining the sales manager's office sat twenty alert, hawk-eyed, ambitious men. Tall and suave men, short and cocky men, thin and waspish men, plump and genial men. Each designed to a different blueprint. But all breathing in a superior brand of oxygen.

"Wanted," the advertisement had pleaded, "Chief Salesman at £1,000 per annum. Must possess initiative and imagination. Live man. Corpses need not apply."

At length the sales manager's secretary popped her pretty head into the waiting-room, and promptly withdrew to put on her Wellington boots. In such an electric atmosphere some form of insulation was called for.

Entering again, she told Applicant No. 1 that the boss would see him now. No. 1 entered the holy of holies with all the assurance of one who in his time had sold as many combs to bald-headed men as he had deck-chairs to people with no gardens.

Applicant No. 2 reckoned he could sell umbrellas in California; No. 3, sunshades in Manchester.

Likewise, Nos. 4 to 20 inclusive were all self-confessed best sellers.

The manager buzzed for his secretary. "I'm darned if I know which one to choose," he admitted. "They're all good."

"Why not give them the direction test?"

"Good idea!" exclaimed the sales manager, for many a smooth talker had stumbled over that.

"Now then," he snapped, as No.1 was re-ushered into the office, "how would you get to the Town Hall from here?"

The applicant scratched his head, for about the first time in his life lost for words.

"Er—you take the first left and second right. No, I'm a liar; it's the first right, second left. Then at the crossroads you take a 99 bus. Or is it a 66 tram?"

To give force to his halting remarks he waved his arms about like a Boy Scout practising semaphore. The manager was unimpressed. "Send in No. 2."

No. 2 got to the Town Hall with the aid of a piece of paper on which he drew a map that was Town and Country Planning at its most futuristic. It might possibly have led the reader into the river; certainly not to the Town Hall.

No. 3 indulged in a bout of ums and ahs, with some hand-waving thrown in. He would have made an admirable windmill but a poor Town Hall director.

By the time it got round to No. 19 the unhappy applicants were practically standing on their heads in a misguided effort to trace a route to the Town Hall. The sales manager himself opened the door to let out No. 19.

Taken by surprise, No. 20 was jet-propelled into the office, the crouching-to-the-keyhole position having given him extra momentum. The manager frowned at the would-be salesman, but was secretly pleased. Here at least was a man with initiative!

"I won't ask you to direct me to the Town Hall," he said cunningly. "Tell me how to get to Mill Street."

Pausing only momentarily, No. 20 rattled off: "First-right-second-left-over-the-bridge." The words staccatoed like a machine gun working overtime. "Then-take-the-left-fork, cross-at-the-lights, then-second-left."

The speaker didn't need to use his hands; they were firmly entrenched in his trousers pockets.

No. 20 got the job. He was a man with initiative *and* imagination. There was no such place as Mill Street in the locality.

To Coin a Phrase

Jaggers, the solicitor, coughed discreetly. "And now, ahem, to the bequests."

Jim Cranbourne nudged his cousin Mary. Broadly translated, the nudge said: "This is what the carrion crows are waiting for. But knowing your dear departed Uncle Roderick, they're in for a shock!"

The corners of Mary's shapely mouth twitched in friendly response to the nudge.

Jaggers paused to polish his spectacles.

The carrion crows fidgeted in their plush nests. They had trains to catch, and were anxious to know whether it was to be first-class return or third.

The solicitor attempted again his delicate task. "And now to the bequests, which the deceased describes as Bequests Extraordinary.... "To my second cousin Amelia, I leave my, ah, National Health glasses, to assist her to see some good in others—"

Amelia, a fat, frustrated fifty, rose. "Come, Percy," she directed her nag-ridden spouse, "It was a waste of time attending the funeral."

Like a marionette operated by remote control, Percy meekly followed his masterful mistress.

"And to my second cousin by marriage, Percy, I leave—"

The departing couple halted by the door.

"—a length of rope, to facilitate towing by the said Amelia. Or for a more useful purpose that might commend itself."

The door slammed.

The long list of bequests followed the same ironic trend.... "To my brother, Humphrey, I leave a window-box and a tobacco plant—my choice cigars being no longer at his disposal.

"To my sister Mildred—who so constantly begged me to provide for her rainy day—I bequeath my old umbrella."

Now Jim and Mary were the only relatives ever to have displayed any real affection for Uncle Roderick. And only to the young couple had the departed Roderick displayed any warmth of feeling.

"To my nephew, James, I leave my lucky silver three-penny piece. Exercising his initiative, this may (to coin a phrase) be magnified a hundred-fold."

Jim smiled wryly. So rusty was his initiative that, as a commercial representative, he had yet to land that sales-managership. Nevertheless, he was three-pence better off than any of the others!

"To my niece, Mary, I bequeath some good advice: marry Jim!"

Mary blushed as Jim nudged her again.

The nudge said: "Look here, Mary! For all his eccentricity, Uncle Roderick was a shrewd old boy. He knew we were childhood sweethearts. It's a pity we only meet on these family occasions. Let's start a family occasion of our own!"

The Bequests Extraordinary having been concluded, Jaggers was more at ease. "Finally, ladies and gentlemen, I understand the deceased disposed of his estate in a separate will—"

The carrion crows looked up expectantly. There might yet be some pickings to take back to their love nests.

"—But unfortunately I was not privileged to draw up the document. In fact, I have no information as to its whereabouts."

The relatives crowed indignantly.

The solicitor smiled for the first time. "However, there is a brighter aspect. Should the will not come to light within one calendar month, the estate will be divided among you all at my discretion. I suggest, therefore, that we adjourn to the dining-room and assemble again at 2 p.m. to discuss a worthy settlement."

Jim Cranbourne pocketed his lucky three-penny piece. He leaned forward to Mary. "We don't want to lunch in that fusty old dining-room," he whispered. There's a cosy little restaurant in the village."

The Acacia Restaurant boasted a cosy alcove, and behind its curtains the young couple were soon enjoying a cosy luncheon.

"Uncle Roderick was quite a card," Mary remarked.

"Card? He was the whole pack of cards! Joker included. The Jack, too, for that matter. In his time Uncle Roderick has been a Jack of all trades—making a tidy pile on each."

"I wonder who gets the money in the missing will," Mary mused. "Certainly not Aunt Maud," she added. "You should have seen her face when Uncle left her a microphone for broadcasting scandal."

Jim grinned. "You should have seen your face, Mary, when you were bequeathed to marry me. You remember I nudged you then. That nudge was a proposal. What d'you say?"

"When?" Mary said simply

"As soon as I can support you on my commercial travelling."

"We can't wait that long, Jimmy. I'll support you on my shorthand-typing."

Jim shook his head reluctantly. "It might not work out."

"Don't forget, Jimmy. We share in Uncle's estate if the will doesn't show up within a month."

"I shouldn't bank on that. Old Jaggers doesn't approve of me; I'll be lucky to chalk up 100 quid."

Mary pouted prettily. "At least it will pay for our honeymoon."

They argued the point throughout the soup course, the meat course, and the sweet. At the coffee stage they were still arguing.

Long past the hour for their due return to the family meeting they were still at it. But Jim was weakening.

"We'll compromise," he said. "Let the lucky three-penny piece decide."

He took the coin from his pocket and spun it into the air with an exaggerated casualness. "Heads we get married soon. Tails, we wait."

The coin hit the raftered ceiling, ricocheted off an electric light bracket, and somersaulted on to the table. Two heads bumped together as their owners studied the upturned surface for a long, long moment.

"Tails," said Mary dejectedly. "We wait."

"Wait!" echoed Jim—but with an optimistic inflection of voice. "You nip back to the family conclave, while I dash along to the jewellers...."

Twenty minutes later he was dashing back into the house. He burst into the study and took his place in the family circle beside Mary.

At his rude entry, the Mildreds and the Humphreys frowned their disapproval. Jaggers, the solicitor, raised an eyebrow.

Mary lowered an eyebrow, to wink at the intruder. "Did you get the ring?" she whispered.

"No, darling. I'll get the ring when I return to the jeweller the object I just borrowed."

Jaggers coughed discreetly. "You are late, Mr. James, and in the absence of your statement of means I have allocated you £100 from the estate."

"You are spared your sub-division, Mr. Jaggers. I can direct you to the will."

The Mildreds gasped. The Humphreys groaned. Jaggers was mystified.

Jim explained. "The spin of the lucky coin gave me the clue. Uncle Roderick said that, exercising my initiative, the coin may be magnified a hundred-fold—to coin a phrase. Well, here is the means of magnification—a glass I have borrowed from the local jeweller."

The bewildered solicitor took the coin and applied the magnifying glass to the inscription on the Tails side.

"Good gracious," he said at length. "This is a properly–constituted will, duly signed and witnessed." He read aloud. "To my nephew, James, I bequeath my entire estate."

Jim Cranbourne nudged his bride-to-be. "The medallion–engraving trade was one of which Uncle Roderick was Jack!"

To the Ends of the Earth

The turquoise-blue of the lake gave way to a dusk-purple, as the setting sun relinquished its sovereignty to the moon.

From her seat by the water's edge, Lynn could see hear the friendly chugging of a lake steamer and the murmur of a miniature waterfall. The lilt of a gay Swiss melody came from the hotel lounge.

She read again the letter she had just written, which formed a signpost at the crossroads to a new life.

I've gone away, Frank. Right out of your life…. She had spent the sleepless train journey across France in seeking the right phrases. She was determined not to hurt Frank….

She could hardly say: "I'm afraid to face you in case you read the truth in my eyes."

If it is any consolation, I want you to remember me always as your friend and admirer.

Slipping the letter into her handbag, Lynn gazed across the lake.

As the lights of the tiny chalets on the far shore lit up one by one, their reflections formed a jewelled cascade on the placid waters.

The accordionist broke into a more plaintive melody, and Lynn felt a catch in her throat. It was *their* tune. "I'll be loving you—always." Tears welled to her eyes.

She hastily brushed them away as she heard footsteps crunching on the gravel path. It was the hotel manager.

Upon her arrival that afternoon she had taken an instant liking to Monsieur Gerard, with his rotund figure, trim white hair and Van Dyck beard. His friendly blue eyes seemed to reflect the wisdom of the ages.

He stood before her and bowed. "Bonsoir. Would Mademoiselle care to join the dancing?"

Lynn smiled. "No, thank you, Monsieur. I'm afraid I'm in no mood for dancing."

"It is a pity, Miss Marchant." The hotelier spread his hands, pleadingly. "We have in the dance tonight many young soldiers. *Les soldats braves* deserve the worthy partner, especially—" he regarded her with an approving eye—"the tall and beautiful brunette."

"I'm sorry, Monsieur. I'm rather tired after my journey."

M. Gerard drew nearer, and after a moment's hesitation sat down on the seat beside her. "Perhaps Mademoiselle is unhappy?"

"Why should I be unhappy," Lynn countered, "when I have come to Switzerland to marry?"

"Tell me more," Gerard invited. "This lucky man, what is he like?"

"Oh, Barry's an angel."

"That I do not doubt. But what manner of an angel?"

"He's an artist."

"Ah, I comprehend. He came to Switzerland to paint this beautiful scenery."

"Well, no. he came for treatment at a sanatorium."

"I'm sorry," said the old man softly.

"But he's better now," Lynn said brightly.

"Then I'm glad."

There was a short silence, and then M. Gerard asked, with gentle insistence, "Do you love this Barry?"

Lynn replied, defensively, "We've been engaged for two years."

"That is no answer—there is perhaps another man in England? Maybe you would like to confide in old Henri."

Coming from anyone else the suggestion would have been impertinent, but this newly-found friend seemed so understanding, and it would be a relief to confide in someone.

So Lynn plunged into her story. How she had met Barry at a party. Carefree, irresponsible Barry, whose zest for living was a foil to her own more placid temperament.

"You see, Monsieur, although that was only two years ago, and I was already in my late twenties, I was inexperienced, naïve. I regarded this as the real thing, and we were engaged after a whirlwind courtship.

"And then he was taken ill, and the doctors ordered him to a sanatorium, and that meant goodbye for a while. In all his letters Barry said that my love was doing more than all the kind nurses to make him better. And then—"

M. Gerard broke in gently: "And then, came this real thing?"

Lynn nodded. "Frank Peterson was a new client I met and—"

"And before that contract was signed, you were negotiating Cupid's business, eh?" M. Gerard interjected.

Lynn smiled wryly. "We both fell in love, but I felt I was pledged to Barry, and that he needed me.

"A few days ago I heard from him. He said he had recovered and would be coming home soon. I had to make a quick decision between the two, and I chose Barry. This meant I had to try to forget Frank completely, so I gave up my job, cashed my savings, and came to Switzerland."

M. Gerard was a sympathetic listener. "Have you never told this Frank that you really love him?"

"How could I? He would have followed me to the ends of the earth. That would have meant hurting him more, because I can't alter my decision."

The old man shook his head. "I see there is no point in trying to make you change your mind. But I do not think you are wise. In my native France one says: *Toujours l'amour*. That is a very good—how d'you say?—motto."

"You are very kind," Lynn murmured. "But this letter I have just written to Frank has sealed the contract."

She took it from her handbag, and said half-defiantly, "I must post it right away."

"In that case, Mademoiselle, I will get you the envelope. One moment."

Gerard rose and went into the hotel foyer.

"And here," he offered on his return, "is the pen also to write the address." He took out his cigarette lighter. "Here is the light to see better. And the stamp. There behind you is the post box. And here is my hand to wish you *bonne chance*."

He shook hands gravely with Lynn, bowed and walked away. Lynn was left to the stillness, the twinkling lights, the murmuring waters, the strains of melody, and to her thoughts....

* * * * * *

The early morning sunlight stole through her bedroom window and beckoned Lynn to awakening. She experienced a delightful feeling of expectation—a warm feeling that reminded her of waking as a child on Christmas Day.

A week had passed since her talk with Gerard, and today she was to see Barry. Her drowsiness was chased away by the thought of being with him again.

She hastened out of bed, and flung the window wide, drinking in the crisp, sparkling air. From a distance came the tinkling of cow bells. To her they were wedding bells, in rehearsal.

After an early breakfast, she set off for the sanatorium. The first stage was a short ride on the quaint, single-decker tramcar which sped past the hotel, and connected with the mountain railway.

The electric train, clean and fresh as the surrounding countryside, wove its way through ever-changing scenery of spell-binding grandeur. And as the train steadily mounted, Lynn's spirits rose with it.

Impatiently she sank back into a corner seat. Her mind flashed to the beginning of an eventful week. Her arrival in this heart-warming country, and that tête-a-tête with M. Gerard. Then the following morning, the telephone call to the sanatorium.

"Hello, Barry," had been her simple greeting. "How are you?"

And Barry's infectious voice, which somehow always seemed to convey the impression of a friendly grin: "LYNN, where are you speaking from?" Then excitedly, "You *can't* be here in Switzerland."

"But I *am*, dear! And we're going to be married soon."

A pause—Barry was evidently letting the idea sink in—and then he said: "I'll have to possess my benighted soul in patience for seven days, darling. That's when I'm being discharged, and they won't allow visitors before that date. Where are you staying?"

"I refuse to tell you," Lynn had laughed. "I'll be waiting at the gates when you come out."

The remainder of their conversation had been an exchange of endearments, which had somehow kept up her spirits throughout the long week of waiting....

And now at last—

It was surprising how she had conditioned her mind, and heart, to the point where she was really anticipating the reunion. Completely and resolutely had she tried to put thoughts of Frank Peterson behind her.

The train jerked to a halt at the little station on the mountain top, and Lynn was brought back to reality.

A ten minutes' walk separated her from the sanatorium. It was grand to be up at the mountain peak. Walking briskly along the narrow road, she drank in the air, as intoxicating as champagne.

Far below, the silver ribbon of road threaded its way through the multi-coloured dress of the countryside. Like the tiny cars, scurrying along antlike, her cares were reduced to minute proportions.

The edelweiss and the blue-belled gentian grew in wild profusion about her, and she picked a posy for the lapel of her trim white suit. She could not resist a glance in her handbag mirror, or a feeling of satisfaction at the way the flowers caught and magnified the blue depth of her eyes.

When she reached the entrance to the hospital drive, Lynn glanced at her watch. Barry had said 3.30. Her eagerness to see him again meant she had over an hour to spare. To her present mood of bubbling anticipation she could not wait that long at the gate. She strolled through the spacious grounds towards the entrance of the building.

Her pace quickened as, in the distance through the trees, she saw the hospital. The drive wound to the right, and as she turned the corner she came upon a couple in a passionate embrace, in a secluded arbour.

Involuntarily, she stopped, as she recognised the broad shoulders and fair hair of Barry—with a nurse!

What Lynn saw was no casual farewell kiss. And obviously not the first, she thought bitterly.

She stood still for what seemed ages in stunned silence—unbelieving.

"Oh! Barry."

His gaze of startled guilt met hers for an instant; then fell before the sorrowful reproof in Lynn's eyes.

She turned and crept back down the path. Tears came unashamedly as she realised that all her plans had collapsed in those last few minutes. Somewhere at the back of her mind was the thought that she ought to be very happy at the unexpected turn of events. Wasn't she now free to marry Frank?

But it was not as simple as that. Two short weeks earlier, after mental torment, she had made a momentous decision, when she had thrown in her job and uprooted herself from home and friends. Most important of all, she had schooled herself to forget that she had ever met Frank Peterson. It had taken a tremendous effort of will, and a suppression of natural instincts.

Despondently, Lynn made her way down the mountain. As she descended, so did her spirits fall.

She supposed things would turn out all right in the end. But how did she approach Frank? Her letter had been so final.

Lynn had lost all count of time, and suddenly she noticed that the evening light was failing. The snow-capped mountains had taken the mantle of dusk about their broad shoulders. Unheeding as she was, an inner instinct warned her of the danger of being lost beneath that dark cloak. So she hurried to join the train at the next boarding point.

There was dancing in the hotel lounge that evening. But Lynn sat on the lakeside verandah, seeing solace from the still waters which had befriended her on the evening of her arrival in this country.

Footsteps crunched on the gravel path. It was the hotel manager.

What a timely meeting. She could confide in Henri.

The wise old gentleman sat beside the bewildered young lady and listened to her story in silence.

"So you see, M. Gerard, fate has been very unkind. My sacrifice was all in vain."

"I would not say that, Mademoiselle. Perhaps he will come back to *you*. Who knows? Perhaps, not believing your letter, he will seek you out in this very hotel? Did you not tell me that he would follow you to the ends of the earth?"

"But that's impossible. I purposely did not give Frank my address."

Henri rose and walked away, chuckling. Puzzled, Lynn watched him disappear into the hotel.

Five minutes later, she heard someone coming. As if by instinct, she rose to greet the newcomer.

"Frank," she breathed, and flew into his outstretched arms "So you *have* come!"

"Yes, darling. M. Gerard said I would find you out here."

"And he was right, bless him. So very right about everything. But how did you know where to find me?"

"That hotel manager is a scheming old rascal," Frank laughed. "The address of the hotel was printed on the back of the envelope he gave you. He knew that all the time!"

Twilight threw its discreet veil about them as they embraced where they stood. In harmony with their attuned hearts, were the strains of melody from the hotel lounge, the friendly chugging of the lake steamer, and the murmuring waters.

There was a brief silence between them as they sought words to bridge the gulf of their recent separation. The accordionist struck up with a melody no longer plaintive: *I'll be loving you— always.*

"Our tune," they said simultaneously, and laughed. The gulf was bridged.

Smiling happily, they swung into the dreamy waltz rhythm.

Turning Worms

Perhaps it was the spaghetti that reminded Inspector Levitt of the "Bilbury Backyard" murder. Association of ideas, and all that.

Anyway, dining as my guest, the inspector was casually forking a wriggly length of spaghetti when he remarked: "Even the worm will turn, you know."

"Out with it!" I invited. "What was the name of the criminal worm who turned?"

"Roderick Glebb was his name," the inspector replied. "The Bilbury Backyard murderer. Proper lady-killer he was. Not, you must understand, in the romantic sense, for he was an insignificant character. Five-foot-six in his elastic-sided boots, and one-foot-nothing in his wife's estimation. Life with the Glebbs was one long round of nagging and yes-me-dearing.

"Now, to the night of the worm-turning. And, incidentally, Roderick's disposal of the body involved the turning of worms, because he decided to dig a hole in the back garden and bury the lady."

The inspector made a ruminative dig at his spaghetti.

"My account of the night's dark deeds must necessarily be sketchy, as I wasn't present," he continued. But based on the evidence and the confession of the accused, it seems the events went something like this:

"Approaching midnight on a moonlit night, Mrs. Waggitt, the Glebbs' next-door neighbour, poked her scraggy head out of her back bedroom and saw Roderick Glebb digging up the geraniums at the bottom of his garden. Now this was surprising, because they were his wife's choice plants.

"Mrs. Waggitt—being the suburb's ace scandalmonger—knew the Glebbs weren't on the best of terms. (Walls have ears in these flimsy houses.) She also knew they had one heck of a row the previous evening. As a matter of fact, Roderick had spoken up for himself, by way of a change. Mrs. Nosey Parker also knew that Mrs.

Glebb had been missing all day, and was stated to have gone to visit relatives in Australia."

The inspector chuckled. "Taken all in all, you can imagine how interesting to Mrs. Waggitt was this spot of midnight gardening.

"Hastily, she put on her dressing gown, her carpet slippers and her new Spring hat, and crept into the garden. There she took a ringside seat behind a blackcurrant bush. The coffin-shaped hole next-door was growing steadily bigger, and piled beside it was a heap of rubble. An hour later the hole assumed life-size dimensions. At that point Glebb paused to mop his brow and rest on his spade— just at the instant when the warted tip of Mrs. Waggitt's nose became visible over the hedge.

"Realising she had been seen, she made a bold face of the situation. 'Good evening, Mr. Glebb,' she said, as casually as she could. 'Gardening?'

"'Uh-huh,' came the reply.

"Mrs. Nosey Parker pointed to the heap of rubble. 'Building a rockery, Mr. Glebb?'

"Roderick nodded again and shovelled the base of the hole to a meticulous flatness.

"'Your wife wouldn't approve of your disturbing her favourite flowers, Mr. Glebb.'

"'My wife has gone to Australia,' Glebb replied curtly.

"'Just think,' Mrs. Waggitt said maliciously. 'As she has gone to the other side of the world, you could say, in a sense, *your wife will soon be underneath that rockery.*'

"'You could say that,' Roderick agreed, calmly."

The inspector paused in his yarn. "Of course, the rockery was a pretty feeble place for hiding a body. It was one of the first places we searched. But turning worms aren't noted for their foresight.

"After Mrs. Waggitt had asked him more pertinent questions, Roderick said: 'Look here, Mrs. Waggitt, can you keep a secret?'

"'Oh yes, Mr. Glebb,' said the suburb's biggest blabber. 'Do tell.'

"'If you want to know the truth of it, Mrs. Waggitt, I was just about fed up with my wife's nagging. I hated her and her confounded geraniums, and I've always wanted a rockery. So this morning I got rid of my wife.'

"'Mr. Glebb! You killed her!'

"'No, I'm sorry to disappoint you. I really did send her to relatives in Australia. What's more, Mrs. Waggitt, I'm fed up with your tittle-tattle. If I started digging at night, I knew you'd be out to watch. This hole is for you!'

"The worm turned, batted the scandalmonger with his spade, and buried her under the rockery."

Urchin Cut

"Spare a copper for the grotter, mister?"

The grotto arrayed on the pavement within a framework of dingy moss, was a magpie miscellany of pebbles and shells, a marble or two, and a jaded dandelion.

In the topmost right-hand corner was a sparking object which had all the appearance of a chip of cut glass.

"Remember the grotter, mister!"

The young speaker reached out a grubby palm. Tod Swanney brushed it aside. He had more important things to think about; notably, how to persuade Lucky Joe to divulge the whereabouts of the Branscombe Diamonds.

Tod walked on for some twenty yards; then stopped as though encountering an invisible brick wall. He had been pulled up by his subconscious mind (always a smarter thinker than his conscious).

That sparkler, whispered Tod's subconscious. Why is it in a kid's grotto, when in could be in your pocket?

In answer to his thoughts, Tod returned to the grotto. Winning the confidence of the two small custodians with a grudging penny apiece, he bent down to inspect the collection. With a clumsy attempt at sleight of hand he pocketed the sparkler.

Finesse was never Tod's strong suit. The smaller boy whimpered. "Martin, the man took our bit of glass."

Tod said hastily, "I'll give you a shilling for it."

Martin took the coin readily and turned to his younger companion. "It's all right, Johnny, there's plenty more glass where we found that bit. Besides, we can buy four lollies with this bob."

Tod walked away, relieved at having avoided a scene. One way and another, he had figured in too many scenes for his comfort.

But once again his subconscious applied the brakes. You heard what the kid said. There's plenty more glass where they found that bit. The Branscombe Diamonds, Tod me boy. The loot that Lucky Joe hid before the cops nabbed him!

So back once more to the grotto. This time Tod flashed a ten shilling note. "The price of 1,000 lollies," he said (with bad arithmetic but good psychology), "if you tell me where you found that bit of glass."

For a seven-year-old, Martin had a good head for business, albeit an ignorance of diamonds. "Okay, mister. We found it under the hedge round the big house across the common. The house with the iron gates."

Tod smiled congratulations to his subconscious. There was only one house in the vicinity answering to the lad's description—Branscombe Manor, from which Lucky Joe had made his successful burglary but unsuccessful escape.

Tod thanked the lad, and made his way to the glittering spot. He thought of Lucky Joe—whose nickname had been blunted by a ten-year jail stretch. Served him right for his meanness. From now on it was to be Lucky Tod, with a 100-per-cent cut from the Branscombe haul instead of a measly five.

The hedge that skirted Branscombe Manor was extensive, under-tended and overgrown. After half an hour's search, the foliage clung to its treasure with the tenacity of an oyster.

From the factory in the locality, came the blast of a siren. Five o'clock. Tod cursed, because it would be getting dark soon. With a lightning decision which he was he pleased to think savoured of Lucky Joe's master-mind, he hastened across the field to the main road.

It was a timely return, for the grotto-keepers were packing their chattels when Tod made his breathless arrival. He flashed a pound note, the last of his capital. "Here you are, son," he said to Martin. "It's all yours if you take me to the big house."

Martin snatched the note, and scooped the contents of the grotto into his smaller companion's pocket. "Take the grotter home, Johnny, and tell Mum I'm running an errand. C'mon, mister!"

Maintaining a nimble pace ill-suited to one of Tod's condition, Martin led the way across the common. Tod stumbled over potholes in the gathering dusk, and only the thought of that 100 per cent cut kept him going.

After the fifth stumble, he asked: "Are you sure we're going the right way, son?"

" 'Course I am, mister. Look! We're there."

A hedge loomed up large in their path. At a point where it joined the iron gates, lay a collection of sparklers brilliant in the blackness.

The youngster picked up a few, then scuttled off home. Tod took an eager step forward to scoop up many.

But again his subconscious held him back. Take a look at what the boy called the big house.

Slowly, Tod looked beyond the hedge and the gate, towards the factory. Its neon sign read: THE ACE COMPANY FOR CUT GLASS.

Vicious Circle

As the train purred into Loughton Station, I dotted the final full stop to my manuscript. Then with a twiddle of the pencil, I made it into a comma; nothing like finishing on an original note.

Another brain child was born! Now to present it to the circle, who, acting as literary midwives, would breathe life into the brat.

It was quite a yarn, I kidded myself. All about a pock-marked Mulatto who had a squint in both eyes, a full set of fang teeth, and a livid scar running from the head of his head to the bottom of his bottom. A cheerful cove, his practice was to rob lonely graveyards at midnight and ship the bodies out to Africa to grace his relatives' dinner table. When he ran out of bodies, he would murder a nice juicy fat man here and there, to supplement the ration.

A winner, I was sure. Try it out on *John Bull* first; failing that, *Listen With Mother*.

Well, I read it to the circle; and as it came to a dramatic close I looked up expectantly. There was an uncomplimentary hush, broken only by the snores of an enterprising member who had gone to sleep.

"Well," said the chairman, the sharpest man who had ever fiddled a sixpenny sub, "What d'you think of that, Miss Phillip-Phlopp?"

"I wasn't listening," she replied. "Frankly, I don't care for that type of story, and my mind wandered halfway through."

(It was a revelation to me that this member *had* a mind.)

"Mr. Rew-barb?"

"Well, I'm afraid it wasn't humorous enough for me. It didn't maintain the pace of the positively scintillating open word. Y'see, after that, we rather expected a wisecrack in every other syllable."

"Mr. Bum-freeze?"

"Too humorous. I was so engrossed in laughing at the gags that I couldn't concentrate on the plot." (It was a recognition, at any rate, that there *was* a plot.)

"Still," he added, "I think Mr. Long-thirst has definitely got something there—and I advise him to take it to the nearest dustbin."

"Mr. Ambone?"

"I don't think it'll get published. I should know because I have a sister-in-law once removed on my step-grandfather's side who works in a newspaper office. I don't think any woman would act as the heroine did, unless she was a man. And as for that part where she sees the Mulatto ripping open his victim with blunt bread-knife, where she screams 'Oh-h-h,' I felt sure she should have screamed 'Ah-h-h.' That alone is good for a rejection slip."

"Mrs. Rew-barb?"

"Too morbid; I don't care for that sort myself. I suggest you change the Mulatto in the graveyard to a fairy at the bottom of the garden."

And so the comments were hurled from all sides. Summarised, it would appear that my story was:

Too short.

Too long. ("Cut out the first 1,000 words"—a bit difficult for a 750-worder.)

Too farcical.

Too morbid.

The ending was too vague; it left the reader in the dark.

The ending was too explanatory. ("Credit the reader with *some* common sense.")

The following points also gave rise to rejection slips:

By my use of the expression "he acted very foolishly," I had touched on insanity. Taboo.

In mentioning the heroine's "former husband" I was suggesting divorce. Taboo.

The "ghost of a smile" savoured of the supernatural. Taboo.

The hero drove along in a car two inches the wrong side of the white line and wasn't sent to prison for it. Offended the moral code. Taboo.

Taken all round, it seemed that the circle had assembled not to cheer, but taboo.

By ten o'clock, I had decided to take up knitting.

However, on the train journey home I got out pencil and paper and rewrote every scene, every sentence, every word.

"Well," my wife greeted me, "what did they think of your latest story?"

"It was a great success," I replied proudly. "Mrs. Linseed liked it very much."

Author's note on title page: "Any resemblance between the characters in this story and any person living, dead or with one foot in the grave is deliberately intentional. The reader may care to identify himself with the characters, but don't plump for the angle character—because that's me." Names hand-written in margins, in order of appearance: Mr. Sharp, Miss Phillips, Mr. Rew, Mr. Humphreys, Mr. Amsden, Mrs. Lindsay.

Without Scruple

I found the lounge empty, save for the eminent novelist, Riverley Winters. His presence was an effective barrier to the seclusion for which the club is noted, but courtesy dictated that I should choose a chair next to him.

"Cheerio, Smithers," he said after a few minutes, but this did not indicate imminent departure;

He was acknowledging the drinks I had seen fit to order. "Here's to the success of my new novel," he went on—toasting himself before the fire of self-adulation. "What did you think of it?"

"A winner," I replied diplomatically. "Although I did hear whisper of an impending libel action."

The author nodded. "What can I do if people choose to ignore that preface about all characters being fictitious? However, libel actions are a great boost to sales." He chuckled wickedly. "I'll tell you how I came to write that novel."

And this is the story behind the story, as told to me in the author's own words.

* * * * * *

I like parties (said Riverley Winters) but parties don't like me—judging by the dearth of invitation cards which find their way through my letterbox. Maybe people find me a crusty old bachelor bore. Which of course I am. Or maybe the eccentric parties who attend these eccentric parties are afraid I'm going to feature them in my next novel. Which of course I am.

At any rate, I hadn't had an R.S.V.P. card for over a year, when out of the blue came an invitation from Mrs. De Lancy de Willoughby to spend a few days at her country home.

Mrs. De Lancy de Willoughby is what is termed "county"—an obscure county in the Midlands, as it happens, but nevertheless county. A widow of 40, she possesses the grand type of beauty which can well afford to admit it is forty. De Lancy de Willoughby is not her real name; it is a snobbish assumption that she regards as more "countyish" than the name her dear, departed father left her, together with a large mansion and no money.

No dove of peace brought a greener olive branch than did the postman with Mrs. de Willoughby's invitation card, for I had fallen out with her some time back when her friends found their way into my novels. Intrigued by her change of heart, and having some time on my hands before starting a new book, I packed my bags at once.

When I arrived, the place was cluttered with young men-about-town trying to look like young men-about-county; debutantes who were due to come out at any time, and were well aware of it; and more matronly types who should have gone in long ago, and who weren't aware of it.

I call them guests, because that's what Mrs. de Willoughby called them. In fact they were lodgers, enjoying the euphemistic title of paying guests. From an author's viewpoint, there was only one of any interest, apart possibly from Mrs. de Willoughby herself, and that was Sir Gerard Haverling.

I've never met a man with a granite jaw, although I used the expression in my apprentice days; and Sir Gerard was the type I should have so described. His jaw was not more solid than mine or yours, but the set of his features gave the impression that it was. Maybe it was the hard glint of his eyes. He wasn't above five foot eight, with breadth of shoulder only in proportion; and yet one had the impression that his immaculate evening jacket was bursting at every seam with suppressed muscularity.

Haverling was a self-made man, they told me. An indeterminate phrase, that, for we are all self-made men—our lives being what we make them. Anyhow, with Sir Gerard it meant that, joining the army as a private, he had reached the heights, had made some good contacts and was now established in big business.

Devoid of scruple, a snare to unsuspecting femininity and gullible investors alike, he had trampled his way through life with hobnail boots labelled, "I'm all right, Jack."

Mrs. de Willoughby introduced him as if exhibiting a pedigree Pekinese. "Oh, Mr. Winters, you must meet the distinguished Sir Gerard Haverling. He's my pet guest."

The accent seemed to be on the word "pet," for Haverling's arm was linked affectionately in that of his hostess as he shook my hand. "A pleasure to meet you, Mr. Winters," he barked (more Alsatian than Pekinese). I hear you're making a good thing out of your writing. Perhaps I could interest you in an investment?"

Mrs. de Willoughby chimed in. "I think I can interest Mr. Winters more in your life story."

Sir Gerard appeared taken aback at this remark, but not more so than was I. It was so unlike Mrs. de Willoughby to intrude on her friends' private lives when I was about.

Nevertheless, the idea had merit....

But I found Haverling to be singularly uncommunicative, once he learned I wasn't talking finance. His manservant, Witton, however, proved to be a fount of information.

I came across Witton in the billiard room one evening, which properly was out of bounds to servants. But I'm not snobbish; students of human nature can't afford to be. 100-up at billiards and a bottle of stout; these were the keys which unlocked Witton's tongue.

He was a nasty individual. If you can imagine a handsome weasel—well, that was Witton. He had been Haverling's batman in the war and was his chauffeur-valet-handyman. A plum of a job by all accounts; it certainly had to be more than loyalty, to retain Witton's services.

This was demonstrated by his opening remark at when we chatted after the game: "Sir Gerard Haverling is a swine," he volunteered.

I raised my brows. It was pointless commenting on the obvious.

"He's trying to take Mrs. de Willoughby away from me."

"So!" I exclaimed. "You are fond of the good lady too."

"And why not? With me and Sir Gerard at the moment it's a sort of Box and Cox game. But I think I'm winning. Mrs. de Willoughby's offered me a nice cushy job, and what's more she says she's going to ask Haverling to leave."

"You'll be sorry to leave Sir Gerard after all this time?" I suggested. "Didn't you see the war through together?"

Witton nodded. "I started as private and finished the same way. Haverling started as private, crawled to Sergeant, wormed his way to Captain, bluffed his way to Major, and shot his way to Colonel."

"*Shot* his way?"

"Nothing less. Colonel Higgins, our Company Commander, stood in the way of Haverling's further promotion. And so—well, the three of us were out on patrol one night and only two came back."

"And Higgins?" I queried.

"Shot in the back."

This was indeed an interesting story, I thought, and might well expand into a novel, wrapped around the unscrupulous character of Sir Gerard Haverling. I was thus minded at the time my visit came to an end. Two later incidents finally formed the scope of my novel.

One: an announcement in the papers of Mrs. de Willoughby's second marriage. And it wasn't to Haverling or to Witton.

Two: news that Mrs. de Willoughby had engaged a new chauffeur-handyman. And it wasn't Witton.

I thought this matter over completely. Then I wrote my book (Riverly Winters concluded). And now South for the libel actions!

* * * * * *

"Has Sir Gerard actually started proceedings?" I asked.

The author laughed. "Good Lord, no. It's obvious you haven't read my novel; Haverling hardly appears in it at all. It's the study of a scheming, unscrupulous woman: Mrs. De Lancy de Willoughby to a T.

"It was she who inveigled Sir Gerard to her house as a paying guest. She who invited me along in the hope that I would meet him, learn his story and disgrace him in a novel.

"She who flirted with Haverling and set him at loggerheads with that weasel Witton, then promised Witton the earth if he disclosed to me Haverling's guilty secret."

"But why, Mr. Winters?" I asked. "Why should Mrs. de Willoughby seek revenge on Sir Gerard?"

Riverly Winters smiled sardonically. "I told you his real name was less 'county' than de Willoughby. She is Mrs. Colonel Higgins."

Worldly Wise

Daft Ernie sat in the bar of the Cat and Canary, his flapping ears missing not a scrap of conversation, his big mouth agape at the wonder of human experience. He was called Daft Ernie because at 30 he hadn't the wit to work for a living: but perhaps it was a moot point!

When the tall but broad-shouldered man walked into the bar, Ernie wasn't the only goldfish; twenty mouths gaped as one mouth. Donkin, the landlord, summed up the situation for the dumbstruck clients: "Lor' luvvus, it's Big Jim Crump! It must be ten years since you walked out of this very pub to buy a packet of fags. We wondered when you was coming back."

Big Jim nodded and proffered his flash cigarette case at large. "Not the same packet I went out to buy," he replied to Donkin's unspoken question. "I've smoked plenty since then—cigars, hookahs, hubbly bubblies, opium. Been all around the world, you know. Australia, China, Africa, South America...."

He rattled off the names as casually as a porter reciting the stations on the slow line to Little Twistleton.

"I suppose my old cottage has been let?" Big Jim went on.

"Yes," Donkin affirmed. "We gave you up after five years. Matter of fact, Farmer Bright keeps a slaughter-house there now."

"You're welcome to buy the property," the famer put in quickly, with an eye to business. "I'll soon clean it up, presentable-like."

"Worth considering," Jim Crump said nonchalantly, twirling his stick; it came within an ace of decapitating Ernie. "I've got the best part of £50,000 put by, you know."

Whistles of admiration gave way to murmurs of appreciation as Jim went on grandly: "It's drinks all around, landlord."

Everybody ordered a pint of ale, with the exception of Ernie, who ordered two pints.

"Tell us what happened," the landlord invited, "from the time you walked out of here."

"I reckon I was drinking that night," Big Jim began, "and had a sudden urge to go to sea. I strolled down to the creek yonder and hopped onto a barge. Mark you, I thought she was bound for Sandport down the river. Turned out to be China.

"I might've nipped off at Hong Kong, but by this time I was onto a nice smuggling racket. So I was aboard for two years, growing fat on the racket and thin on the rations. In the end, they threw the cook overboard."

Daft Ernie, who of all the agog listeners was the agogest, remarked here: "Murder in the galley! I can see it all."

"It was murder all right," Big Jim agreed, "and I was having no part of it. I skipped off at Singapore and made my way to Australia. Took up kangaroo farming; training the blighters to box. You may have heard of Killer Kane, the Kangaroo Kid—entered him for the lightweight championship. Sad business that: had to withdraw; couldn't make the weight.

"Next stop South America: little republic of San Calvador. Got mixed up in a revolution there and when the last shot had died away, found I was president. Quite a paying game, though somewhat uncomfortable. I survived it for a year and then crossed the border two seconds in front of a bullet."

"A runaway president," guffawed Daft Ernie, who had steadily been growing agoger and agoger. "I can see it all."

He wished he had the means to travel to them foreign parts. It wasn't that he didn't enjoy having nothing to do all day, but would have preferred to do that nothing in more exciting surroundings.

"Runaway is right," said Big Jim. "I reckon I ran all the way to Africa. It was quieter in the jungle. Bumped into a tribe there who made me the god of Heat Waves. Got fed up in the end and cashed in my baubles at the nearest trading post. I was worth £20,000 by the time I reached India...."

And so the travelogue went on, and by the time Jim Crump had made £100,000, which he had decided to come home to spend, the landlord was making a mental note to order a bigger cash register.

After closing time, Daft Ernie strolled along the village streets, meditating with a degree of concentration which his fellows would have said was impossible for him. How he wished he could travel to the places described by Big Jim!

He had reached the slaughterhouse where the traveller's cottage had once stood, when he saw the renowned raconteur in person.

"Good evening," Jim greeted. "Thought I'd give the old place the once-over, you know. Goodnight!"

Ernie didn't take the hint, but said, slowly: "I don't reckon you've travelled *so* far, Mr. Big Jim. I've seen all the things you spoke of at the Picture House. Good films, they was—Runaway President, Murder in the Galley, and I don't know what else."

Jim laughed uncertainly. "So you suppose I saw those films too?"

Ernie nodded. "I reckon they have film shows in prison, which is a place they hold a man for ten years."

"So what? Mr . Clever Daft Ernie!"

"So I reckon the loot you're digging up here was what you got sent to prison for pinching. And I reckon that half of that 100,000 will take me round the world, where I won't see no policeman to tell on yer."

Winter Comes Too Soon

They sat in the study adjoining the surgery; the fair-haired young artist and the grey-haired family doctor. After seating his patient in an easy chair, and before pronouncing his fateful verdict, Dr. Medlow had opened the brandy. The measure he poured for himself was, if anything, the more generous of the two; it was no light task to usher out of this world a young man he had ushered in only 25 years ago.

"You asked for the truth," said the doctor. "Very well. I'll give you twelve months to live."

Adrian Stone laughed, but his tones had a false ring—the polite uncertainty of a listener who didn't really see the joke. "You'll give me twelve months?" You sound more like a judge than a doctor."

Medlow said nothing. He could think of nothing to say.

Adrian, too, was silent a while. And then: "Don't tell Estella," he pleaded. "There are some things even a wife shouldn't know."

"If you wish it—" the doctor began.

"Don't tell Estella. Ha, ha, that sounds like a music hall number!" Adrian hummed a few bars of a popular song, fitting in his own words to the melody. "Don't tell Estella, old fella, don't tell 'er...."

"Here, fill your glass again, my boy." There was no accounting for the reaction to shock; in Adrian's case it seemed to have exaggerated his sense of humour.

Adrian filled his glass, took a long pull at his cigarette, and then the earnestness that never lurked far beyond the pallour of his classic features, came to the fore. "Forgive the outbreak, doctor. But seriously, don't tell Estella; it would spoil things for the rest of my... my life."

"You mean you'd be unhappy together?"

"On the contrary, we are unhappy *now*. But if Estella knew, she would feel compelled to do everything to make me happy. She would sacrifice all her principles and all her persuasions on the altar of sympathy."

"And what may I ask, are they?"

"Principles? Estella is convinced I'm not a good artist, on the evidence of my not having ranked an Academy showing."

"Nonsense!" the doctor broke in. "She is entertaining a genius unawares!"

"And persuasions?" Adrian went on. "She is always battening on to me to give up painting for a more paying proposition. If she guessed the truth about my condition, she would leave me in peace. Our bickering would cease, but it would be a synthetic brand of happiness. I don't want emotional charity."

Adrian smiled ruefully. "Being a lover of beauty, I was captivated by her looks. I don't blame her for not sharing my temperament."

Dr. Medlow drained his glass slowly, and with a lightening of mood said: "Enough of this probing into your private life…. Now, tell me how are you going to spend the year which lies before you?"

The doctor's casual question set off a spark within Adrian. He stood up, clenched a slim fist and banged on the table. "I'm going to paint," he said. "To paint, d'you hear me?" The emotion behind his words lent colour to his normal pallour, and his eyes shone like signal lamps on a dark highway. "I'm going to paint, and paint." His fists drummed out a tattoo on the table-top. "To paint… to paint."

* * * * * *

Two months later Adrian called again on Medlow. "You won't need the stethoscope, doctor. I've come for a chat, not a check-up."

"And how's the painting coming along?" Medlow asked with a twinkle. "Have you finished any new work?"

"I've finished twenty."

"Have you sold any?"

"None. Luckily, I have a private income."

"H'm. The so-called experts are obviously only so-called!"

"I can't altogether blame them. My work has been shoddy of late. I've been so anxious to get so much done in so little time that I've skipped from picture to picture—doing justice to none."

"But you've found a remedy. I can see it in your eyes."

"You're right, sir, and that's why I'm here. I just had to tell someone, and of course I can't confide in Estella."

"Spring will be upon us soon, doctor, and *Spring* will be the title of my next canvas. I'm taking a cottage down in Radshire. The village of Silent-Waters-by-the-Glade boasts a stretch of scenery the like of which, for a springtime setting, you could search all England in vain.

"Then, when Summer comes, I'm off to Birchfield, for a *Summertime* canvas."

"And in Autumn," the doctor said, swept along by the young man's enthusiasm, "what about Brierly Parkside?"

"An ideal spot for *Autumn*," Adrian agreed. "I know it well. Then a suitable spot for *Winter*, and my programme will be complete. It's symbolic, don't you see, Dr. Medlow. Nature is born, flourishes and dies in one brief year. I'll accompany nature along its course, and at the end of the year I too shall die. The portrayal of the Seasons will be my life's work."

* * * * * *

Silent-Waters-by-the-Glade was all that Adrian had rated it to be. From a hillock on the outskirts of the village, where the artist had pitched his easel, there stretched a panorama that was nature's mute poem. The emerald glade bedecked with the early wild flowers, the woodland trees whose young shoots kicked their way into life, and through the middle of the glade, the silver lake whose waters had been washed crystal clear by the winter rains.

At peace with the world, and with himself, Adrian feasted on the scene with the hungry greed of a genius—his brush flowing across the canvas in inspired strokes. Even Estella had to admit, on his nightly returns to the cottage, that the picture was "taking fair shape."

The calendar pursued its relentless course, and his first canvas was packed safely away. Summer beckoned Adrian to Birchfield, to paint the second.

But although the summer scene was captured with equal skill, he did not now earn Estella's grudging praise. They were staying at a small guest house in the country town, and she yearned for the life of the nearby seaside resort.

"Why don't you pack up that painting?" she asked one day. "You'll never make a name for yourself. Not, if you do, until after you're dead."

Adrian was silent. How could he rebuke Estella? Fate, not she, had added the sting to the remark.

"Well, if *you* choose to mope about all day, Adrian, *I* don't. I'm packing my bags, and you can join me any time you like at the Imperial Hotel on the promenade."

And so Estella left for the grandeur of the Imperial Hotel. Adrian remained in his small guest house, satisfied with the grandeur of Nature. Nothing would be allowed to detract him from his painting. Nothing!

He sat alone at dinner that evening, and having finished his meal, was idly sketching on the menu card. His conscious thoughts were, as always, directed towards his painting, but subconsciously he was observing the queer little man who sat at the table opposite. He wasn't above five feet tall, and he reminded Adrian's subconscious of a gnome.

After a while the stranger rose and came to Adrian's table. "D'you mind if I share my coffee with you?" he asked. His air of authority belied his appearance.

"Please do."

The little man leaned across to study the artist's sketches, and seeing the result, chuckled. "A good likeness," he commented.

"Eh, what?" Coming out of his trance, Adrian was horrified to note the effect his doodling had. He had faithfully reproduced the old man's elfin features, but had added a picturesque beard and pixie hat.

The old man cut short his apologies, and immediately introduced the subject of artistry in general, Adrian's own work in particular.

With all the force of a visionary, Adrian held forth. "Come to my room," he said at length, "and I will show you the picture I'm working on."

"There!" he said, unwrapping the painting, in his voice all the pride of a mother exhibiting a new born infant. "D'you like it?"

"It's wonderful. I should like to see the finished work."

Adrian beamed, an expression which grew deeper as the stranger went on: "I should like to give you a commission."

"You will buy my 'Four Seasons' when they are finished?"

"Not exactly."

Adrian's face fell.

"Here is my card."

Despondently, Adrian read the printed pasteboard: *The Mammoth Publishing Co.—James A Willington, Proprietor*. "So," he said flatly, "a commercial job."

"Don't speak so disparagingly, young man. We are shortly producing a series of children's books, and your elfin sketches are just what we want. And that's not all. You can handle our Christmas card illustrations."

"I couldn't do it at any price, Mr. Willington."

"Not at my price?" Mr. Willington named a figure which made Adrian whistle.

"Not even at that price. It would be prostituting my art."

The old man shrugged. "I'll leave you my card, and if you change your mind don't forget to ring me. It's an easy number—Silverstone 1-2-3-4."

* * * * * *

The weeks sped by. Back home again with Estella, Adrian was looking forward to an early commencement of his Autumn canvas.

The telephone rang to distract his thoughts. It was his solicitors.

"This income of yours, sir; I'm afraid you won't get much more out of it. The bottom's fallen out of the shares market."

"I see," said Adrian dully. He didn't really see, for he had no head for business. And certainly he didn't see his way ahead without money. He had enough perhaps to see him through the rest of his short life whilst he finished his paintings; but what of Estella when he had gone?

Perhaps the way *was* clear to see; at least the line of duty was.

Suddenly he felt very tired, and very ill.

He picked up the telephone. "Operator, I want Silverstone 1-2-3-4."

* * * * * *

Adrian worked like a draught horse during the next few weeks, at which time he was able to send the first proofs to Mr. Willington.

They came back by return of post. "Sorry to return these," Mr. Willington wrote. "They are far below standard. You once made slighting remark about commercial art; but even prostitutes give value for money, you know. You can do better than this. You *must* do better than this."

The publisher was right, of course. He must abandon all efforts at painting until he had honoured his commercial contract.

"Thank you for your revised work," Mr. Willington wrote later. "It was a masterpiece."

Christmas Eve came upon him before Adrian had started his Winter landscape, and he planned to get started as soon as he could escape the festivities.

On Christmas morning two letters were predominant on the hall table. One contained a Christmas card addressed to Adrian from his friend Dr. Medlow. The illustration on the card was one of Adrian's own design. The other envelope contained a cheque—a handsome cheque—from the Mammoth Publishing Company, by way of first royalties.

But Adrian was not fated to see either document. During the night his soul had passed beyond, to the Great Academy, there to present the canvas of his earthly deeds to the Supreme Artist.

His life's work was done.

12112320R10117

Made in the USA
Lexington, KY
19 October 2018